喚醒你的英文語感！

Get a Feel for English !

喚醒你的英文語感 ！

Get a Feel for English !

愈忙愈要學
英文提案與報告

行 **500** 大企業的 *Leximodel* 字串學習法

BIZ ENGLISH
for
BUSY PEOPLE

由數千篇商務提案與報告中
彙整出高頻字串，不必抄範本！
不必學文法！！
只要熟悉本書蒐羅的 52 個語庫，
提案報告一次過關！

貝塔語言出版
Beta Multimedia Publishing

作者⊙商英教父 Quentin Brand

Contents

目錄

Part1 · 撰寫英文提案

Unit 1. 令人印象深刻的英文提案

Unit 2. 情況概述

Unit 3. 提出建議

Part 2 · 撰寫英文報告

Unit 5. 如何寫出效果佳的英文報告

Unit 6. 專案進度報告

Unit 7. 聯繫報告

Contents

目錄

前言

The Leximodel

引言與學習目標

從亨利‧福特（Henry Ford）到雅詩蘭黛 (Estée Lauder)；從史帝夫‧賈伯斯 (Steve Jobs) 到傑克‧威爾許 (Jack Welch)，所有登上成功高峰的企業強人都有三個共通點：1. 具備洞察需求的慧眼，看得到別人看不出來的需求；2. 能想出創意十足又可行的點子來滿足需求；3. 具有說服力，可讓他人接受點子並貢獻專門知識（know-how）跟挹注資金，讓想法能夠實現。當然，除此之外，他們也有決心、勇氣、經驗、專業能力，和無數個焚膏繼晷的夜晚！

雖然大多數人不是雅詩蘭黛或史帝夫‧賈伯斯，商場上的成功關鍵卻都部分植基於這三個能力：洞察需求的能力、想出好點子來滿足需求的能力，以及說服他人你的想法行得通的能力。

雖然前兩項能力多半會隨著年齡的增長、閱歷，以及在職場和工作上豐富的歷練而與時俱進，但基本上它們還是與生俱來的。你或許可以洞察出他人看不到的需求，也可能不行；你或許有好點子來改變事物，也可能沒有。然而，倘若你無法說服別人接受自己的意見，那麼徒具這兩種能力也無用武之地。說服他人接受你的遠見，信任你並投注他們的時間、金錢和資源在你的想法上，這個能力是絕對可以透過學習而獲得的。其實這個能力說穿了就是有效的溝通——有效地使用溝通工具來傳達你的想法。而商業提案和商業報告便是幫助你實現有效溝通的工具。

本書旨在幫助你撰寫說服力十足和令人印象深刻的英文提案和報告，同時也透過簡單而實際的研讀法門，幫助你提升一般的英語能力。

現在請花點時間看看下列的問題，並寫下你的答案。先做這個 Task，不要看其他內容。做完後再往下看。

TASK 1

想想這些問題，並寫下自己的答案。

1. 你為什麼購買這本書？
2. 你想從書中學到什麼？
3. 你在寫英文提案和報告時遇到哪些困難？

看看以下這些針對上述問題所提出的可能答案，勾選和你的想法最接近的答案。

1. 你為什麼購買本書？
- ☐ 我買這本書是因為我想學習對工作有幫助的英語。
- ☐ 我真的忙得不得了。我不想浪費時間去學工作上用不到的東西，或是練習在職場中派不上用場的語言。
- ☐ 我知道報告或提案的寫作技巧跟電子郵件的不一樣，我已經買了這個系列中關於寫電子郵件的書，不過我需要知道如何寫報告和提案。
- ☐ 我想學進階的商業寫作技巧。
- ☐ 我想要一本透過練習來引導的書，同時還要有簡單的參考要點。這本書可以讓我隨身攜帶與查閱，就像一本專為商業寫作所寫的英文字典。
- ☐ 我想要一本了解我想要什麼的書！

2. 你想從書中學到什麼？
- ☐ 我想學到我最常要用到的字彙和文法，來處理我的商業事務。
- ☐ 我想要學到組織提案或報告架構的正確方式。
- ☐ 我希望這本書告訴我我錯在哪裡，並加以改正。我希望這本書就像是我的私人語言家教。
- ☐ 我覺得自己寫提案和報告的文筆一定很乏味，因為每次都是同一種寫法和文字用到底。我想學到如何豐富文字。
- ☐ 我英文念得不太好，而且很討厭文法。我覺得文法很無聊，而且比在一群老外前做簡報還可怕！可是我也知道，文法非懂不可。所以我希望可以不必學一大堆文法，就可改善我的商業寫作技巧。
- ☐ 我想找到靠自學來改善英文的方法。我在說英語的環境中工作，但我知道自己沒有善用這個優勢來培養專業的英文能力。我希望這本書能告訴我怎麼做到這點。

3. 你在寫英文提案和報告時遇到哪些困難？

❑ 我不確定提案中應該包含哪些資訊，還有內容應該有多詳細。我也不確定哪種提案架構最好。我寫報告時也有相同的疑慮。

❑ 我知道若想讓別人採納我的提案，文字精準很重要，但是我不知道該如何改善文筆。我找不到其他可以教我做到這一點的書。

❑ 我高中時代學過的英文文法已全部還給老師，要是當時上課專心一點就好了！

❑ 有時候我怎麼都想不出貼切的用詞或用語，總是辭不達意。

❑ 每次寫提案或報告都得花上很長的時間，我真的很想更有效率一點，好把時間花在其他事情上。

❑ 文法、拼字你想得到的，我樣樣不行！

你可能同意以上這幾點的部分或全部，你也可能有其他我沒有想到的答案。不過先容我自我介紹。

我是 Quentin Brand，我教了十五年的英文，對象包括來自世界各地的商界專業人士，就像各位這樣，而且有好幾年的時間都待在台灣。我的客戶包括企業各個階層的人，從大型跨國企業的國外分公司經理，到擁有海外市場的小型本地公司所雇用的基層實習生不等。我教過初學者，也教過英文程度非常高的人，他們都曾經表達過上述的心聲。他們所想的事和各位一樣，那就是要找一種簡單又實用的方法來學英文。

各位，你們已經找到了！這些年來，我開發了一套教導和學習英文的方法，專門幫像各位這樣忙碌的生意人解決疑慮。這套辦法的核心概念稱作 Leximodel，是以一嶄新角度看語文的英文教學法。目前 Leximodel 已經獲得全世界一些最大與最成功的公司採用，以協助其主管充分發揮他們的英語潛能，而本書就是以 Leximodel 為基礎。

本章的目的在於介紹 Leximodel，並告訴各位要怎麼運用。我也會解釋要怎麼使用本書，以及要如何讓它發揮最大的效用。看完本章後，各位應該就能：

❑ 清楚了解 Leximodel，以及它對各位有什麼好處。

❑ 了解 chunks、set-phrases 和 word partnerships 的差別。

❏ 在任何文章中能自行找出 chunks、set-phrases 和 word partnerships。
❏ 清楚了解學習 set-phrases 的困難之處，以及要如何克服。
❏ 清楚了解本書中的不同要素，以及要如何運用。

但在往下看之前，我還是要先談談 Task 在本書中的重要性。各位在前面可以看到，我會請各位停下來先做個 Task，也就是針對一些練習寫下一些答案。我希望各位都能按照我的指示，先做完 Task 再往下看。

每一章都有許多 Task，它們都經過嚴謹的設計，可以協助各位在不知不覺中吸收新的語言。做 Task 的思維過程比答對與否重要得多，所以各位務必要按照既定的順序去練習，而且在完成練習前先不要看答案。

當然，爲了節省時間，你大可不停下來做 Task 而一鼓作氣地把整本書看完。不過，這樣反而是在浪費時間，因爲你要是沒有做好必要的思維工作，本書就無法發揮最大的效果。請相信我的話，按部就班做 Task 準沒錯。

The Lexmodel

可預測度

在本節中，我要向各位介紹 Leximodel。Leximodel 是看待語言的新方法，它是以一個很簡單的概念為基礎：

Language consists of words which appear with other words.
語言是由字串構成。

這種說法簡單易懂。Leximodel 的基礎概念就是從字串的層面來看語言，而非以文法和單字。為了讓各位明白我的意思，我們來做一個 Task 吧，做完練習前先不要往下看。

TASK 2

想一想，平常下列單字後面都會搭配什麼字？請寫在空格中。

listen _____

depend _____

English _____

financial _____

你很可能在第一個字旁邊填上 to，在第二個字旁邊填上 on。我猜得沒錯吧？因為只要用一套叫做 corpus linguistics 的軟體程式和運算技術，就可以在統計上發現 listen 後面接 to 的機率非常高（大約是 98.9%），而 depend 後面接 on 的機率也差不多。這表示 listen 和 depend 後面接的字幾乎是千篇一律，不會改變（listen 接 to；depend 接 on）。由於機率非常高，所以我們可以把這兩個片語（listen to、depend on）視為固定（fixed）字串。由於它們是固定的，所以假如你不是寫 to 和 on，就可以說是寫錯了。

不過，接下來兩個字（English、financial）後面會接什麼字就難預測得多，所以我猜不出來你在這兩個字的後面寫了什麼。但我可以在某個範圍內猜測，你在 English 後面寫的可能是 class、book、teacher、email、grammar 等，而在 finan-

cial 後面寫的是 department、news、planning、product、problems 或 stability 等。但我猜對的把握就比前面兩個字低了許多。爲什麼會這樣？因爲能正確預測 English 和 financial 後面接什麼單字的統計機率低了許多，很多字都有可能，而且每個字的機率相當。因此，我們可以說 English 和 financial 的字串是不固定的，而是流動的（fluid）。所以，與其把語言想成文法和字彙，各位不妨把它想成是一個龐大的字串語料庫；裡面有些字串是固定的，有些字串則是流動的。

總而言之，根據可預測度，我們可以看出字串的固定性和流動性，如圖示：

The Spectrum of Predictability 可預測度

字串的可預測度是 Leximodel 的基礎，因此 Leximodel 的定義可以追加一句話：

Language consists of words which appear with other words. These combinations of words can be placed along a spectrum of predictability, with fixed combinations at one end, and fluid combinations at the other.

語言由字串構成。每個字串可根據可預測度的程度區分，可預測度愈高的一端是固定字串，可測預度愈低的一端是流動字串。

Chunks、Set-phrases 和 Word Partnerships

你可能在心裡兀自納悶：我曉得 Leximodel 是什麼了，可是這對學英文有什麼幫助？我怎麼知道哪些字串是固定的、哪些是流動的，就算知道了，學英文會比較簡單嗎？別急，輕鬆點，從現在起英文會愈學愈上手。

我們可以把所有的字串（稱之爲 MWIs = multi-word items）分爲三類：

chunks、set-phrases 和 word partnerships。這些字沒有對等的中譯，所以請各位把這幾個英文字記起來。我們仔細來看這三類字串，各位很快就會發現它們真的很容易了解與使用。

我們先來看第一類 MWIs：chunks。Chunks 字串有固定也有流動元素，listen to 就是個好例子：listen 的後面總是跟著 to（這是固定的），但有時候 listen 可以是 are listening、listened 或 have not been listening carefully enough（這些是流動的）。另一個好例子是 give sth. to sb.。其中的 give 總是先接某物（sth.），然後再接 to，最後再接某人（sb.）。就這點來說，它是固定的。不過在這個 chunk 中，sth. 和 sb. 這兩個部分可以選擇的字很多，像是 give a raise to your staff「給員工加薪」和 give a presentation to your boss「向老闆做簡報」。看看下面的圖你就懂了。

⬤ 部分為 fixed　　⬤ 部分為 fluid
（本書各類語庫會依顏色深淺區隔其流動性程度）

相信你能夠舉一反三，想出更多例子。當然，我們還可以把它寫成 give sb. sth.，但這是另外一個 chunk。它同樣兼具固定和流動的元素，希望各位能看出這點。

Chunks 通常很短，由 meaning words（意義字，如 listen、depend）加上 function words（功能字，如 to、on）所組成。相信你已經知道的 chunks 很多，只是自己還不自知呢！我們來做另一個 Task，看看各位是不是懂了。務必先作完 Task 再看答案，千萬不能作弊喔！

TASK 3

閱讀下列短文，找出所有的 chunks 並畫底線。

Everyone is familiar with the experience of knowing what a word means, but not knowing how to use it accurately in a sentence. This is because words are nearly always used as part of an MWI. There are three kinds of MWIs. The first is called a chunk. A chunk is a combination of words which is more or less fixed. Every time a word in the chunk is used, it must be used with its partner(s). Chunks combine fixed and fluid elements of language. When you learn a new word, you should learn the chunk. There are thousands of chunks in English. One way you can help yourself to improve your English is by noticing and keeping a database of the chunks you find as you read. You should also try to memorize as many chunks as possible.

【中譯】

每個人都有這樣的經驗：知道一個字的意思，卻不知道如何正確地用在句子中。這是因為每個字都必須當作 MWI 的一部分。MWI 有三類，第一類叫做 chunk。Chunk 幾乎是固定的字串，每當用到 chunk 的其中一字，該字的詞夥也得一併用上。Chunks 包含了語言中的固定元素和流動元素。在學習新字時，應該連帶學會它的 chunk。英文中有成千上萬的 chunks。閱讀時留意並記下所有的 chunks，將之彙整成語庫，最好還要盡量背起來，不失為加強英文的好法子。

答案 ▶

現在把你的答案與下頁語庫比較。假如你沒有找到那麼多 chunks，那就再看一次短文，看看是否能在文中找到語庫裡所有的 chunks。

提案與報告 必備語庫 前言 1 ▶

• be familiar with n.p. ...	• every time + n. clause
• experience of Ving ...	• be used with n.p. ...
• how to V ...	• combine sth. and sth. ...
• be used as n.p. ...	• elements of n.p. ...
• part of n.p. ...	• thousands of n.p. ...

• there are ...	• in English ...
• kinds of n.p. ...	• help yourself to V ...
• the first ...	• keep a database of n.p. ...
• be called n.p. ...	• try to V ...
• a combination of n.p. ...	• as many as ...
• more or less ...	• as many as possible ...

★ 📂 語庫小叮嚀

◆ 注意，上面語庫中的 chunks，be 動詞以原形 be 表示，而非 is、was、are 或 were。

◆ 記下 chunks 時，前後都加上 ...（刪節號）。

◆ 注意，有些 chunks 後面接的是 V（go、write 等原形動詞）或 Ving（going、writing 等），有的則接 n.p.（noun phrase，名詞片語）或 n. clause（名詞子句）。我於「本書使用說明」中會對此詳細說明。

好，接下來我們來看第二類 MWIS：set-phrases。Set-phrases 比 chunks 固定，通常字串比較長，其中可能有好幾個 chunks。Set-phrases 通常有個開頭或結尾，或是兩者都有，這表示完整的句子有時候也可以是 set-phrase。Chunks 通常是沒頭沒尾的片斷文字組合。Set-phrases 本質上比較是在交際時使用的用語，也就是說可用來達到某個目的，例如在餐館點菜、寫電子郵件請對方幫忙、或者在講話時澄清誤解。提案和報告因為，描述性較高之故，因此比較少會見到 set-phrases，不過部分章節還是會用到一些，我在第二、三、四章中會教你。現在請看下列語庫並做 Task。

TASK 4

請看下頁提案和報告中使用的 set-phrases，請把你認得的勾選出來。

提案與報告　必備語庫 前言 **2** ▌▶

- From our experience, ...
- It is proposed that + n. clause
- It is suggested that + n. clause
- My proposal here is for n.p. ...
- My proposal here is that + n. clause
- My proposal here is to V ...
- My recommendation here is for n.p. ...
- My recommendation here is to V ...
- My suggestion here is for n.p. ...
- My suggestion here is that + n. clause
- These strategies will ensure that + n. clause
- This recommendation will facilitate sb. in Ving
- This will result in n.p. ...

★ 🗁 語庫小叮嚀

◆ 由於 set-phrases 是三類字串中最固定的，所以各位在學習時，要很仔細
地留意每個 set-phrases 的細節。稍後對此會有更詳細的說明。

◆ 注意，有些 set-phrases 是以 n.p. 結尾，有些則是以 n. clause 結尾。稍
後會有更詳細的說明。

　　學會 set-phrases 的好處在於，使用的時候不必考慮到文法。你只要把它們當作
固定的語言單位背起來，原原本本地照用即可。本書的 Task 大部分和 set-phrases
有關，我會在下一節對此有更詳細的說明。但現在我們先來看第三類 MWIs：word
partnerships。

　　這三類字串中，word partnerships 的流動性最高，其中包含了二個以上的意義
字（不同於 chunks 包含了意義字與功能字），並且通常是「動詞 + 形容詞 + 名詞」
或是「名詞 + 名詞」的組合。Word partnerships 會隨著行業或談論的話題而改變，
但所有產業用的 chunks 和 set-phrases 都一樣。舉個例子，假如你是在製藥業服
務，那你用到的 word partnerships 就會跟在資訊業服務的人不同。現在來做下面的
Task，你就會更了解我的意思。

21

TASK 5

看看下列的各組 word partnerships，然後將會使用這些 word partnerships 的產業寫下來。請見範例。

1.

- government regulations
- drug trial
- patient response
- hospital budget
- key opinion leader
- patent law

產業名稱： _____醫藥界_____

2.

- risk assessment
- non-performing loan
- credit rating
- share price index
- low inflation
- bond portfolio

產業名稱： _____

3.

- bill of lading
- shipment details
- customs delay
- shipping date
- letter of credit
- customer service

產業名稱： _____

4.

- latest technology
- user interface
- system problem
- repetitive strain injury
- input data
- installation wizard

產業名稱： _____

答案 ▶

2. 銀行與金融業
3. 外銷 / 進出口業
4. 資訊科技業

假如你在上述產業服務，你一定認得其中一些 word partnerships。

現在我們對 Leximodel 的定義應要修正了：

Language consists of words which appear with other words. These combinations can be categorized as chunks, set-phrases and word partnerships and placed along a spectrum of predictability, with fixed combinations at one end, and fluid combinations at the other.

語言由字串構成，這些字串可以分成三大類 ── chunks、set-phrases 和 word partnerships，並且可依其可預測的程度區分，可預測度愈高的一端是固定字串，可預測度愈低的一端是流動字串。

新的 Lexmodel 圖示如下：

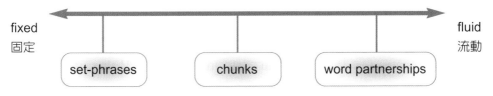

學英文致力學好 chunks，文法就會進步，因為大部分的文法錯誤其實都是源自於 chunks 寫錯。學英文時專攻 set-phrases，英語功能就會進步，因為 set-phrases 都是功能性字串。學英文時在 word partnerships 下功夫，字彙量就會增加。因此，最後的 Leximodel 圖示如下：

The Spectrum of Predictability 可預測度

```
   functions        grammar        vocabulary
      |                 |               |
fixed ←————————————————————————————————————→ fluid
固定                                           流動
      |                 |               |
   set-phrases        chunks      word partnerships
```

　　Leximodel 的優點以及其對於學習英文的妙用，就在於說、寫英文時，均無須再為文法規則傷透腦筋。學習英文時，首要之務是建立 chunks、set-phrases 和 word partnerships 的語料庫，多學多益。而不是學習文法規則，並苦苦思索如何在文法中套用單字。這三類 MWIs 用來輕而易舉，而且更符合人腦記憶和使用語言的習慣。本節結束前，我們來做最後一個 Task，確定各位對於 Leximodel 已經完全了解。如此一來，各位就會看出這個方法有多簡單好用。在完成 Task 前，先不要看語庫。

TASK 6

請看下列文章和翻譯，然後用三種不同顏色的筆分別將所有的 chunks、 set-phrases 和 word partnerships 畫底線。最後請完成下表。請見範例。

　　These days, while many companies in China, Taiwan, Hong Kong, Singapore, and South Korea are trying to find ways to raise capital, many of their counterparts in Thailand, Malaysia, and Indonesia are still trying hard to pay off their debt.

　　Three and a half years after the regional financial crisis, many companies in Southeast Asia are still restructuring their businesses to strengthen their balance sheets. A majority have sold or shut their non-core or non-profitable units to raise funds, while others are negotiating with scores of creditors to extend their loan repayment period.

　　For a good example, look no further than Thailand's Silom City Holdings, Inc., which was once one of the country's most heavily indebted companies. Now, however, Silom owes creditors just

US$110 million, a far cry from the US$542 million it owed at the end of 1997. Its sales and profits last year were US$322 million and US$21 million respectively.

Described by its peers as a model for Thailand's debt restructuring effort, Silom City Holdings sold US$917 million worth of non-core assets by 2000, among them its sanitary goods, electrical products, and packaging units, to raise cash. At the same time, it also sold a 25 percent stake to the Swiss company Wunderbar in exchange for funding and management assistance to help revitalize the company.

【中譯】

近來正當中國、台灣、香港、新加坡和南韓的許多公司全力以赴提高資本的時候，在泰國、馬來西亞和印尼的公司卻仍在絞盡腦汁想法子償還欠債。

區域性金融風暴事過境遷三年半後，東南亞有許多企業仍在重組其企業結構，強化資產負債表。大部分的企業已經賣掉或關閉非核心或無營利的單位，以籌募資金，其他的則忙著與大批的債權人協商，企圖延長還款期。

近在咫尺的泰國 Silom 城市控股有限公司，就是一個很好的例子。這家企業曾是泰國負債最多的公司之一，然而現在 Silom 僅積欠債權人 1 億 1 千萬美元，與在 1997 年底積欠的 5 億 4 千 2 百萬美元相差甚遠。去年該公司的銷售額和營利分別為 3 億 2 千 2 百億美元與 2 千 1 百萬美元。

Set-phrases	Chunks	Word Partnerships
• *For a good example, look no further than …*	• *… try to …*	• *raise capital*

答案 ▶

請以下列語庫核對答案。

提案與報告 必備語庫 前言 **3** ▶

Set-phrases	Chunks	Word Partnerships
• For a good example, look no further than … • At the same time, …	• … try to … • … these days … • … pay off … • … negotiate with … • … scores of … • … one of the … • … a far cry from … • … at the end of … • … a model for … • … sell sth. to sb. … • … in exchange for …	• raise capital • find ways to • regional financial crisis • balance sheets • raise funds • loan repayment period • debt restructuring effort • non-core assets • sanitary goods • electrical products • packaging units • raise cash • management assistance

★ 📁 語庫小叮嚀

◆ 你會注意到這篇文章中只有兩個 set-phrases。這是因為 set-phrases 在本質上屬於交際用語，而這篇文章描述性質較高，交際性質較低。

◆ 注意，set-phrases 通常是以大寫字母開頭，或以句點結尾。而刪節號（…）則代表句子的流動部分。

◆ 注意，chunks 的開頭和結尾都有刪節號，表示 chunks 大部分為句子的中間部分。

◆ 注意，word partnerships 均由意義字組成。

◆ 注意，find ways to 是多重組合 MWIS：ways to V 是 chunk，因為 ways 後面幾乎永遠要接 to V。而 find ways 是 word partnership，因為 ways 可和其他動詞放在一起，find 和 ways 兩者也都是意義字。因此這裡的 word partnership 是由一個動詞和一個 chunk 組合而成。這種多重組合的 MWI 可以說是很稀鬆平常。

　　假如你的答案沒有這麼完整，不必擔心。只要多練習，就能找出文中所有的固定元素。不過你可以確定一件事：等到你能找出這麼多的 MWIs，那就表示你的英文已經達到登峰造極的境界了！很快你便能擁有這樣的能力。於本書末尾，我會請各位再做一次這個 Task，以判斷自己的學習成果。現在有時間的話，各位不妨找一篇英文文章，像是以英語為母語的人所寫的電子郵件，或者雜誌或網路上的文章，然後用它來做同樣的練習。熟能生巧哦！

本書使用說明

　　本書介紹很多在提案和報告中最常使用的固定語言（chunks、set-phrases 和 word partnerships，但絕大多數為 chunks），並說明要怎麼學習與運用。本書也會教各位要怎麼留意每天都可以看到的語言，以及記下這些語言的方法。

為什麼要留意字串中所有的字，很重要嗎？

　　不知道何故，大多數人對眼前的英文視而不見，分明擺在面前卻仍然視若無睹。他們緊盯著字詞的意思，卻忽略了傳達字詞意思的方法。每天瀏覽的固定 MWIS 多不勝數，只不過你沒有發覺這些 MWIs 是固定、反覆出現的字串罷了。任何語言都有這種現象。這樣吧，我們來做個實驗，你就知道我說的是真是假。請做下面的 Task。

TASK 7

看看下列的 set-phrases，並把正確的選出來。

> · Regarding the report you sent me ...
> · Regarding to the report you sent me ...
> · Regards to the report you sent me ...
> · With regards the report you sent ... ...
> · To regard the report you sent me ... ...
> · Regard to the report you sent me ... ...

　　不管你選的是哪個，我敢說你一定覺得這題很難。你可能每天都看到這個 set-phrase，但卻從來沒有仔細留意過其中的語言細節。（其實第一個 set-phrase 才是對的，其他的都是錯的！）說到這兒，我要告訴你學習 set-phrases 時的第一個忠告：

　　雖然各位應該要加強注意所接觸到的語言，但仿效的文字必須以出自母語人士之手為限，像是美國人、英國人、澳洲人、紐西蘭人、加拿大人或南非人；其他人則不夠可靠。絕對只能選擇以英文為母語的人為仿效對象。所謂「英文為母語的人士」，指的是有受過教育的美國人、英國人、澳洲人、紐西蘭人、加拿大人或南非

人，但不一定是白人。如果英文非母語，就算是老闆寫的也不可完全信任。公司中若有人在十年前到美國念過博士，英文能力公認好得沒話說，也信不過。要特別注意：有部分英文為母語的人士的英文很不可靠，就如同很多國人的中文很不可靠一樣。所以你起碼要選擇受過高等教育的母語人士，或已經建立品牌的英文出版物。

無論如何，只能仿效英文為母語人士所寫的文字。

　　如果多留意每天接觸到的固定字串，久而久之一定會記起來，轉化成自己英文基礎的一部分，這可是諸多文獻可考的事實。刻意注意閱讀時遇到的 MWIs，亦可增加學習效率。Leximodel 正能幫你達到這一點。

需要小心哪些問題？

　　本書中許多 Task 的目的，即在於幫你克服學 set-phrases 時遇到的問題。學 set-phrases 的要領在於：務必留意 set-phrases 中所有的字。

　　從 Task 7 中，你已發現自己其實不如想像中那麼細心注意 set-phrases 中所有的字。接下來我要更確切地告訴你學 set-phrases 時的注意事項，這對學習非常重要，請勿草率閱讀。學習和使用 set-phrases 時，需要注意的細節有三大類：

1. **短字**（如 a、the、to、in、at、on 和 but）。這些字很難記，但是瞭解了這點，即可以說是跨出一大步了。Set-phrases 極為固定，用錯一個短字，整個 set-phrase 都會改變，等於是寫錯了。
2. **字尾**（有些字的字尾是 -ed，有些是 -ing，有些是 -ment，有些是 -s，或者沒有 -s）。字尾改變了，字的意思也會隨之改變。Set-phrases 極為固定，寫錯其中一字的字尾，整個 set-phrase 都會改變，等於是寫錯了。
3. **Set-phrases 的結尾**（有的 set-phrases 以 n. clause 結尾，有的以 n.p. 結尾，有的以 V 結尾，有的以 Ving 結尾），我們稱之為 code。許多人犯錯，問題即出在句子中 set-phrases 與其他部分的銜接之處。學習 set-phrases 時，必須將 code 當作 set-phrases 的一部分一併背起來。Set-phrases 極為固定，code 寫錯，整個 set-phrases 都會改變，等於是寫錯了

　　教學到此，請再做一個 Task，確定你能夠掌握 code 的用法。

TASK 8

請看以下 code 的定義，然後按表格將詞組分門別類。第一個詞組已先替你找到它的位置了。

- **n. clause** = noun clause（名詞子句），n. clause 一定包含主詞和動詞。例如：I need your help.、She is on leave.、We are closing the department.、What is your estimate? 等。

- **n.p.** = noun phrase（名詞片語），這其實就是 word partnership，只是不含動詞或主詞。例如：financial news、cost reduction、media review data，joint stock company 等。

- **V** = verb（動詞）。

- **Ving** = verb ending in -ing（以 -ing 結尾的動詞）。以前你的老師可能稱之為動名詞。

- bill of lading
- customer complaint
- decide
- did you remember
- do
- doing
- go
- great presentation

- having
- he is not
- help
- helping
- I'm having a meeting
- John wants to see you
- knowing
- look after

- our market share
- your new client
- see
- sending
- talking
- we need some more data
- wrong figures
- you may remember

n. clause	n.p.	V	Ving
	• *bill of lading*		

答案 ▶

請以下列語庫核對答案。

提案語報告　必備語庫　前言**4** ▶

n. clause.	n.p.	V	Ving
• you may remember	• bill of lading	• help	• helping
• we need some more data	• wrong figures	• do	• knowing
• did you remember	• customer complaint	• see	• doing
• John wants to see you	• our market share	• look after	• having
• I'm having a meeting	• your new client	• decide	• sending
• he is not	• great presentation	• go	• talking

★ 語庫小叮嚀

　◆ 注意 n. clause 的 verb 前面一定要有主詞。

　◆ 注意 n. p. 基本上即為 word partnerships。

　　所以總而言之,在學習 set-phrases 時,主要會碰到的問題有:

1. 短字

2. 字尾

3. Set-phrases 的結尾

　　不會太困難,對吧?

如果沒有文法規則可循,我怎麼知道自己的 set-phrases 用法正確無誤?

　　關於這點,讀或寫在這方面要比說來得容易。說話時要仰賴記憶,所以這當然會有點困難。不過,本書採用了一項工具來幫各位簡化這個過程。

　　學習目標記錄表。本書的附錄有一份「學習目標記錄表」。各位在開始拿本書來練習前,應該先多印幾份學習目標記錄表。由於要學的 set-phrases 和 word part-nerships 有很多,可以選擇幾個來作重點學習。利用記錄表,把你在各章的語庫中想要學習的用語記下來。我建議每週 10 個。

　　與其擔心出錯，以及該用或違反哪些文法規則，不如參照本書語庫裡的用語，熟能生巧。現在請做下面的 Task，不要先看答案。

TASK 9

請看下面句子中的錯誤，並與前言語庫 2 中的 set-phrases 作比較。請研究這些錯誤，並寫出正確的句子和錯誤原因的編號 (1. 短字；2. 字尾；3. Set-phrases 的結尾)。請看範例 A。

A. From our experiences, this usually works.
　　From our experience, this usually works. (2)

B. My proposal here is for we change suppliers.

C. This recommendation will facilitate our customers at collecting their goods.

D. My recommend here is to increase the price by 2%.

E. My suggestion here is that price reduction.

F. This will result on a cost saving.

G. It is suggest that we start as soon as possible.

答案 ▶

B. My proposal here is that we change suppliers. (3)
C. This recommendation will facilitate our customers in collecting their goods.
(1)
D. My recommendation here is to increase the price by 2%. (2)
E. My suggestion here is for price reduction. (3)
F. This will result in a cost saving. (1)
G. It is suggested that we start as soon as possible. (2)

　　如果你的答案與上述的範例答案截然不同，請再回頭把本章節詳讀一遍，並特別

注意 Task 8 和對於 set-phrases 細節三個問題的解說。這些規則也適用於 chunks。

　　本書有許多 Task 會幫各位將注意力集中在 set-phrases 的細節上，你只須作答和核對答案，無須擔心背後原因。

本書的架構為何？

　　這本書分成兩部分：第一部分教提案寫作，第二部分則教報告寫作。這兩個部分均有一個導讀的章節，談撰寫提案或報告時應有的有效寫作原則，告訴你該如何架構提案或報告、裡面應該包含何種資訊，以及寫作的過程為何。

　　第一部分的重點是提案的架構，第二部分的重點則是不同種類的報告。我會這樣分配，是因為不論你提出什麼計畫，大部分的提案還是會遵循相同的架構，或者至少具備相同的元素。然而報告的種類就多了，這個差別從第二部分的目錄即可略知一二。報告的架構和提案的大致雷同，因此希望你可以將第一部分習得的知識應用在第二部分中。

　　現在請花點時間看看目錄，以熟悉即將展開的學習旅程。

　　第三部分則是 word partnerships 語庫表，我將提案和報告中常用的 word part-nerships 集結成一個個語庫表，並依主題來分類，分別有銷售、生產製造、行銷、財務、人員跟管理，你可以隨時分開研讀。

　　每個章節也都有範例提案或報告，這些都是很好的範本，可多看多學。這些範例沒有被翻譯成中文，因為中文和英文的報告和寫作風格差異很大，我不希望你花太多時間看中文翻譯。不過為了幫助你理解範例內容，我們仍然提供了中文的背景說明和內容摘要，難度高的詞也於該頁下方的 Word List 中作註解。

　　除了各大章之外，書末附錄一提供了各章節「提案／報告必備語庫」一覽表，在你撰寫報告或提案時可當作參考工具使用。

我如何充分利用本書？

　　在此有些自習的建議，協助各位獲致最大的學習效果。

　　1. 請逐章逐節看完本書。為了提供更多記憶 MWIs 的機會，本書會反覆提到一

些語言和概念，因此倘若一開始有不解之處，請耐心看下去，多半念到本書後面的章節時自然就會恍然大悟。

2. 每看完一個章節，就把以前寫過或現在正在寫的一些報告和提案列印出來，重新閱讀一次，看一看哪些地方有錯，並修正錯誤。

3. 建議你用鉛筆做 Task，若寫錯了，還可擦掉再試一次。

4. 做分類 Task 時（請見第三章 Task 3.2），在每個 MWI 旁做記號或寫下英文字母即可。但是建議有空時，還是將 set-phrases 抄在正確的一欄中。還記得當初是怎麼學中文的嗎？抄寫能夠加深印象！

5. 利用書末附錄的「學習目標記錄表」追蹤自己的學習狀況，並挑選自己要用在報告或提案的用語。選擇的時候，不妨記住以下重點：
   - 選擇困難、奇怪、或新的用語。
   - 如果可以的話，避免使用你已經知道、或覺得自在的用語。
   - 特意運用這些新的用語。

6. 如果你下定決心要進步，建議你和同事組成 K 書會，一同閱讀本書和做 Task。

在我開始之前有沒有什麼需要知道的事情？
Yes. You can do it!

翻開第一章前，請回到前言的「學習目標」，勾出自認為達成的項目。希望全部都能夠打勾，如果沒有，請重新閱讀相關段落。

祝學習有成！

Part 1

撰寫英文提案

Proposal

Unit 1
令人印象深刻的
英文提案

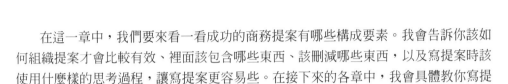

引言與學習目標

在這一章中,我們要來看一看成功的商務提案有哪些構成要素。我會告訴你該如何組織提案才會比較有效、裡面該包含哪些東西、該刪減哪些東西,以及寫提案時該使用什麼樣的思考過程,讓寫提案更容易些。在接下來的各章中,我會具體教你寫提案時可使用的語言,讓你的提案更具說服力,進而提高計畫被接受的機會。

本章結束時,各位應達成的「學習目標」如下:

❏ 更清楚知道有哪些不同種類的需求。
❏ 更了解提案的寫作過程。
❏ 更了解寫提案時該蒐集哪些資料、如何衡量資料的重要性,以及如何呈現資料。
❏ 更清楚知道提案的三大要素。
❏ 更清楚知道提案成功的秘訣。

洞察需求

　　我在前言中提到，成功的秘訣之一，就是有能力洞察出他人看不出來的需求。針對不同的需求得寫不同的提案，因此就這點而言，先了解一下商場上可能遇到的需求將可事半功倍。所有的需求大致上可分為兩類：1. **內部需求**，也就是來自公司內部的需求；2. **外部需求**，也就是來自顧客，以及公司外部、對自己的工作有影響的事業體的需求。現在，就讓我們來進一步探討這兩種需求。

　　內部需求從較不重要的到影響深遠的都有。較不重要的需求包括**設備與資源**——或許你覺得換新的影印機長遠來說有助於公司省錢，或者你想在工作團隊中增雇一名人手；**程序**——或許你看到公司中有些程序缺乏效率，稍加改變後可節省金錢和資源。談到比較重要的需求，則包括**產品**——或許你看到市場或你的產品／服務的範圍中有一個缺口，推出新產品可彌補這個缺口。

　　接著我們來談一談影響深遠的需求，這種需求在公司較高層級中比較會遇到：**行銷計畫**——你得為一個產品或服務研擬行銷計畫，這個計畫必須非常周詳，內含 SWOT 分析、計畫時間表、成本效益分析；最後，你遇到影響最深遠的需求可能就是**商業策略**——或許你覺得公司應該和某個競爭對手合併，或者轉向海外市場或將生產營運遷到另一個國家。

　　現在談一談外部需求，談到這兒就不得不提**顧客**了——或許你覺得一個稍微不同的服務或產品可能更適合顧客，或者你看到一個機會，如果顧客增加購買量，你們雙方都可省成本；另外還有和**供應商**有關的需求——或許你發現供應商目前賣給你的原料有些地方需要改進，或者你需要降低供貨成本；此外，其他的外部需求則可能來自**政府或規範機關**——或許你認為目前政府的相關規定對你產品範圍的限制很多，有礙競爭，希望規定放寬一點。

　　不同的需求需要有不同的提案，因此提案的複雜度和詳細度也不一，此外，針對不同需求所寫的提案，目標讀者也不同，因而所使用的語言也有差異。在深入細談這些問題之前，請先花一點時間看下面的圖。

TASK 1.1

想一想最近寫過的一份提案或自己認為察覺到的需求。此項提案或需求應該歸在圖的哪一個區塊中？內容該有多詳細，寫作對象又是哪類讀者？

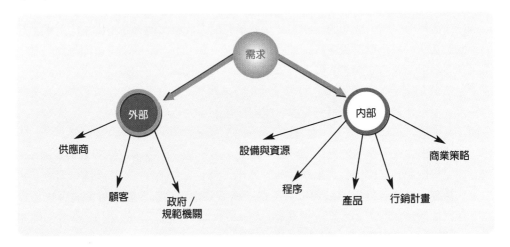

答案 ▶

無論需求是什麼、提案應有多詳細、還有目標讀者是誰，所有提案的元素都跟目標一樣，就是要說服讀者。此外，寫出最後成品——也就是提案時，中間必經的過程也都一樣。

提案的寫作過程

　　提案的寫作過程大致上可分為三個階段：蒐集資訊、衡量資訊以及呈現資訊。我們來逐一探討各階段。

● 蒐集資訊

　　蒐集資訊時需要考慮的問題有三：一、我在提案中該放進哪些資訊，以呈現需求？二、我的提案如何解決需求？三、我該如何說服讀者接受我的提案？這一切請從竭盡所能地蒐集資訊做起。實際上你可能不會在提案裡用上所有蒐集到的資訊，但資料的蒐集和研讀的過程有助於你成為事情現狀的專家，提案才會更有力。你找的資料應該跟需求如何影響公司營利和效率有關。如果有的話，你可以蒐集數據資料，以及統計形式的量性證據，但別忘了也找一些觀察而來的證據。此外，你也可以研究其他公司解決這個需求的方法、研究競爭對手，並盡力蒐集相關的市場資訊。

● 衡量資訊

　　衡量資訊時，需要思考的主要問題為：我該如何說服讀者接受我的提案？這個階段中一個有用的作法，就是思考讀者在看提案時會提出哪些問題，然後在提案中放進問題的答案，搶先制止疑問。同樣地，你應該思考讀者對你的提案可能有的反對意見，並在提案中放進的解決方法，先發制人。在考慮該放進哪些資訊時，請試著想像自己是讀者。若你能說服讀者你已經就事情的現狀作了多方的考量，那麼讀者就較可能採信你的意見。提案中的資訊量應該恰到好處，一方面盡量放入相關資訊，給讀者一個完整的概念，但同時又不至於因為資訊過多，讓提案顯得冗長。你可能會發現有些蒐集到的資訊其實用處不大，但請保留這些資訊，因為日後可能會派上用場。

● 呈現資訊

　　寫提案時，我們先從點出需求、找出滿足需求的辦法出發。然而，為了讓提案更具說服力，很重要的一點就是把提案融入情境中，詳盡的描述背景狀況，以便清楚地讓讀者知道需求在哪裡，以及你的提案可如何滿足這個需求。當你做到這幾點之後，便應該盡量用簡單的方式來呈現。不過，請務必將實際的狀況考量進去，並把焦點放在執行面上。為了幫助你學會這個技巧，我教你一個有用的口訣，叫做 3P：People、Price、Procedure。

● People（人）

　　執行計畫時，領導人是誰？團隊的成員有哪些人？為什麼你選擇這些人加入團隊？還有哪些部門會參與？這些部門參與這個計畫，對他們自己的工作量和效率有何影響？

● Price（價錢）

　　公司必須投入多少資金執行你的計畫？機會成本有哪些？公司執行計畫後會得到多少實際利潤；又會得到多少隱形利潤，如：公關或更高的媒體曝光率？

● Procedure（程序）

　　執行計畫的時間表為何？誰在何時要做什麼事？為了確保計畫能成功並按時執行，有哪些制約辦法？如果計畫拖延，又有哪些懲罰辦法？

　　呈現計畫之後，接下來就應該評估計畫帶來的影響。你得描述採納提案會帶來哪些結果，也應敘述不採納提案會有哪些結果。你應該思考採納或不採納提案的優點和缺點。你必須仔細計算成本和收益，確認他們均正確無誤。你可能得在提案中放進兩三個不同的財務狀況——最佳狀況、最差狀況、最可能的狀況，並談到每個狀況會帶來什麼樣的結果。此外，你也需要做 SWOT 分析（Strengths/Weaknesses/Opportunities/Threats，強弱優劣分析），並且評估競爭對手和市場可能出現的反應。

　　最後，開始寫提案時，你應該思考提案的呈現樣貌和形式。要用簡報的方式呈現嗎？還是寫成報告？如果選擇寫成報告，內容該有多長？你要用何種裝訂方式？封面要放什麼樣的設計？簡報非常重要，因為讀者從中得到的第一印象就是你對提案的認真度和對自己計畫的堅持度。許多公司已有自己的提案範本，因此你只要把內容放進去即可。

　　不管提案的樣貌和呈現方式為何，語言的素養和精準度不容小覷。然而就公平性而言，你希望讀者以提案的內容來評斷優劣，而非你用來傳達訊息的語言素養。但是在現實當中，不管喜不喜歡，你的語言素養確實會影響讀者對你的提案的反應。拙劣的文法、不精準和不恰當的用語，以及大量語意不清的內容，都將讓讀者留下負面印象，破壞提案的說服力。

　　提案的每一個過程都很重要，務必悉心完成，因爲這不只可增進提案的說服力，也可能在寫作過程中，由於發現了某項原因，致使計畫可能行不通，有可能是成本太高，或許是公司沒有能力執行等。如果情況眞是如此，你應該擱置計畫。畢竟，指出一個需求後卻提出一個註定會失敗的計畫，這對自己的事業和聲名無疑是致命的一擊。

　　不過，所有付出過的努力並不會白費。做了這麼多的研究，你對市場會有更清楚的瞭解；此外，思考過 3P 和評估過計畫之後，你已是更優秀的商業人士了。這一切都將更加豐富你的商務經驗。

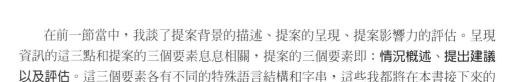

提案的要素

在前一節當中，我談了提案背景的描述、提案的呈現、提案影響力的評估。呈現資訊的這三點和提案的三個要素息息相關，提案的三個要素即：**情況概述、提出建議以及評估**。這三個要素各有不同的特殊語言結構和字串，這些我都將在本書接下來的三章中教你。

如同我之前所說的，無論你要處理的是什麼需求，或者要寫哪一類的提案，或長或短、影響程度或高或低，更無論讀者是誰，所有提案都應包含這三大要素。你可將這些要素當作是組織提案的架構，若是以公司範本寫提案，你也必須確實掌握各個要素所牽涉到的用語。

本章含有大量的閱讀和見解，不管你商務經驗的層級為何，希望你看了之後覺得有趣和實用。建議你先花一點時間重新思考所看過的內容，再繼續看下一章。在本章結束前，請回到引言中的學習清單，確定每一項都確實理解了。

Unit 2
情況概述

引言與學習目標

　　本章的學習目標是撰寫情況概述。我在上一章中也提過，務必把情況完整的交代清楚，此外，更要強調與想法有關聯的地方。情況概述就像是提供提案情境的小型報告，正因為如此，你在這一章所學的時間用語，會跟報告寫作較有關聯。千萬不要小看這一點，學習本章和本書第二部分的時候都要牢記在心。時間用語是提案或報告中不容忽視的部分，很多人在使用動詞時態時也經常感到力不從心，因此本章的篇幅會比其他章長。建議你將本章分段學習，才不會感到無趣。

　　情況概述應該具備三個部分。第一部分應該是對情況過去背景的簡述。第二部分應該是對現況的描述，包括目前趨勢、目前的優勢或弱勢為何。第三部分則應該是對情況未來發展的描述。至於每個部分該有多詳細呢？這得視你的提案類型和想法影響層面的深廣而定。

　　由於情況概述裡的三個部分跟不同的時空有關──過去、現在、未來，因此本章的重點會放在動詞時態的運用。本章有些動詞時態的概念或許會和你之前學到的不大一樣，但無論如何，希望在本章結束時，你對英文動詞時態的理解會比現在更清楚！

　　本章結束時，各位應達成的學習目標如下：

- ☐ 總體來說，對動詞時態及其意義有更清楚的瞭解。
- ☐ 更瞭解自己在使用動詞時態時會有的問題，以及如何避免這些問題。
- ☐ 對提案或報告中不同的部分該用哪些動詞時態有更清楚的瞭解。
- ☐ 能夠更準確的描述過去、現在與未來的情況。

時態概論

我們就先從動詞時態的概念開始談起。

TASK 2.1

請想一想在使用英文動詞的時候，你有哪些不懂的地方和用法上的問題。請在紙上做筆記。

答案 ▶

一般人在使用動詞的時候，最棘手的問題應該就是時態了。英文的時態複雜又特殊，再加上，若不瞭解時態的特質和何時該使用什麼時態時，更會覺得時態很複雜。其實文法觀念錯誤，通常是因為之前的教學法或學習法不對，或是受到了中文動詞的干擾。在接下來的章節裡，希望你敞開心胸，必要時，試著改變對動詞時態的既有概念。為幫助你了解動詞時態，我將教你三個關鍵概念。掌握了這三個概念，理解和使用動詞將會變得更輕鬆。

關鍵概念 1 ▶

我們來看一下中文和英文動詞的差異。中文動詞只傳遞一件訊息，而英文動詞則可傳遞二件訊息。從中文動詞中，我們能看出發生了何種行為，但從英文動詞裡，我們非但可以看出發生的行為，另外還可看出行為發生的時間。此外，在中文裡，我們必須透過句中的時間用語去瞭解行為發生的時間，少了時間用語，便無從得知行為是何時發生的。因此，關鍵概念一要教你的就是：

在英文裡，讀者可從動詞的時態得知行為發生的時間。

關鍵概念 2 ▶

想一想自己對時空的概念，請問時間可分成幾種？大部分的人會說三種：過去、現在和未來。目前為止這樣說是對的，但還有一種時間是大部分人都忽略的，那就是「不受限」的時間。很多時候我們講的事情都與時間無關，意即這些事情並不會受限於特定時間。如：「台灣是一座島。」、「我不喜歡喝茶。」、「你喜歡棒球嗎？」等。

　　瞧，這些都是和時間沒有關係的例子。「台灣是一座島」這件事跟今天、明天或昨天的時間都沒有關係。有些人碰到過去或現在時間的用語也感到頭大。但我們換一個角度思考，就會知道過去的時間是已經結束的時間，而現在的時間是尚未結束的時間。換句話說，昨天已經過去了；今天則尚未結束。一旦這四種時間的概念都清楚了，接下來就只要掌握每個時態代表哪一個時間就行了。因此，關鍵概念二為：

英文有四種時間——不受限、現在時間、過去時間、未來時間。

關鍵概念 3 ▶

時態的專有名稱多半和時態的意義關係不大，這樣說可能不容易瞭解。舉例而言，沒有時間性的時間都是以簡單現在式（present simple）的時態表示。看到這個時態的名稱，大家會以為是和現在的時間有關，這麼說其實只對了一半。大部分時候，簡單現在式描述的是不受限於特定時間的事情。

　　另一個讓人頭大的就是現在完成式（present perfect），看到這種時態大家大多以為描述的是過去的事情，其實也不然。現在完成式是描述發生在現在，但卻尚未結束的行為。因此，關鍵概念三為：

在英文裡，時態的專有名稱經常無法清楚地反應時態的意義。

　　為了總結在前面學到的知識，並讓你更了解時態的概念，請研讀下面的表格。

時間範圍	時態名稱	提案和報告中的使用方式	範例
不受限	• 簡單現在式（沒有時態）	• 永恆不變的事實 • 看法	• Good marketing <u>moves</u> more product than good design <u>does</u>. • Time <u>is</u> money. • Your proposal <u>is</u> quite sensible.
現在	• 現在進行式 • 現在完成式 • 簡單現在式	• 目前一般可見的商業趨勢 • 目前尚未結束的銷售或專案成果 • 目前的情況或局勢（但並非永恆不變的）	• The economy <u>is improving</u> slowly. • We <u>have achieved</u> all our targets this quarter. • Taiwan <u>has</u> roughly 18 million consumers.
過去	• 簡單過去式	• 歷史背景 • 公司歷史上的關鍵事件 • 已結束的銷售或專案成果	• He <u>started</u> the company in 1887. • Sales for last year <u>were</u> excellent.
未來	• 各種不同的時間用語（包括現在式）	• 計畫和預定的事件 • 未來展望	• The new CEO <u>is arriving</u> next week. • The economy <u>is expected to</u> grow by 2% next year. • If our competitors <u>lower</u> their prices, we'll have to follow suit.

　　上述表格旨在建立你對時態的初步概念，裡面的細節我待會兒在本章裡會有詳細的解說。

　　在「過去時間」的欄位中，我並沒有把過去進行式 (past continuous)，如：I was walking.，以及過去完成式 (past perfect)，如：I had walked. 包含進去。這是因為提案或報告的寫作時很少用到這兩種時態，所以你可以略過這部分。好消息一樁，對吧！

　　在繼續深入探討本章的其他章節前，我們先做一個 Task，鞏固學過的知識。

TASK 2.2

請閱讀下面的情況概述及內容,並在所有動詞下畫底線,區分出他們所屬的時間並填入其後的表格中。

【背景說明】

　　GCI 集團是一家位於台灣的家具製造公司和供應商,已有十年歷史。該公司在中國、泰國和台灣都設有工廠,市場遍佈亞洲。他們正積極地快速擴張版圖,企圖成為亞洲市場的龍頭。GCI 集團的策略有兩個層面,第一,開發新的市場和產品;第二,併購小型區域內的競爭對手。目前他們也正試著打進美國市場。公司最近剛在台灣證券交易所上市,為這個擴張策略挹注了更多的資金。公司的行銷部門主管寫了一篇市場上的情況概述給董事會和股東,說明為打進美國市場的行銷計畫,如下。

　　GCI Group acquired Topron PLC last year, in a move that was regarded by many shareholders as controversial. The new group was renamed GCI International. 2,000 staff members were laid off and considerable cost savings were made as a result. New products were introduced at the end of last year to extend the System 99 seating range. In addition, several factories in China and Thailand were modernized. Although their temporary closure while modernization took place had a negative effect on production volume, results began to show some improvements towards the end of the year.

　　This year the merged company has experienced a year of consolidation and growth. GCI International have traded well in the four Asian regions. The new product range has positively affected this year's sales. Market conditions in China and South Korea have been very favorable and results have been excellent there, too. Results

 W o r d　L i s t

acquire [əˋkwær] v. 取得;獲得
PLC (public limited company) (英國的)股份
有限公司
controversial [͵kɑntrəˋvɝʃəl] adj. 有爭議性的

modernization [͵mɑdənəˋzeʃən] n. 現代化
consolidation [kən͵sɑləˋdeʃən] n. 合併;聯合
favorable [ˋfevərəbl] adj. 順利的

from China and Thailand have almost reached the same level as two years ago before the modernization. The Taiwan company is continuing to develop new markets, particularly in the south of the island.

Market conditions were not so favorable in the U.S. last year, but there has been some improvements there this year. The new product line is very attractive, and our market research suggests that its suitability for the U.S. market means that we can expect growth there next year. The figures for YTD show that this growth is already starting to happen.

The outlook for next year is positive in all regions. China and Thailand are tipped to bounce back and start showing some steady increase in production volumes. Our investment in the new plant is expected to start showing some return towards the second half. Sales personnel in these regions will probably be increased to ensure that stepped-up production does not result in increased inventory costs. The China market in particular is ready for expansion in the run up to the Olympics in 2008, and we envisage a steep growth curve there. In Taiwan, the group looks set to gain the market lead island wide, while next year also looks like being a good year for Korean expansion. We estimate that the U.S. market will develop slowly in the first half, with an increase in new customer orders towards the second half as our marketing efforts begin to take hold there.

【內容摘要】

GCI 集團去年收購 Topron 的舉動引起相當大的爭議，兩千名員工被資遣，但也因此節省了不少人事成本。在去年底，除了有新產品上市外，幾間中國和泰國的工廠

 W o r d   L i s t

YTD (year-to-date) 從年初到現在
be tipped to 被預測會⋯⋯
personnel [ˌpɜsn̩'ɛl] *n.* 全體職員；全體成員

inventory [ˈɪnvənˌtorɪ] *n.* 存貨；商品、財產等目錄
envisage [ɪnˈvɪzɪdʒ] *v.* 預見；預期
steep [stip] *adj.* 急劇升降的

也正走向現代化，雖然因此要關場一段時間，對生產量會有影響，但在年底前，現代化的成效就會慢慢顯現出來。

經過了整合和成長的一年後，GCI 國際集團的新產品在今年的銷售上成績亮眼，中國和南韓的市場狀況也都很發展得順利，成績也很好。台灣分公司在南部市場也發展得不錯。

去年在美國的狀況可就沒這麼順利了，但仍算有些進展。市調顯示新產品很適合美國市場，明年可能會看到成長的狀況，不過年初到現在的數字早已顯示出成效。

明年各地區的前景均一片看好，中國和泰國的市場預計會有回彈的狀況，產量會開始穩定地增長，對新廠房的投資也預計在第二季可以看到成效。這些地區的銷售人員也許需要增加，確保大量生產後不會造成太大的庫存成本。我們預計中國市場在 2008 年的奧運前置作業中會有大幅度的成長。在明年的展望中，台灣和韓國的前景也一片看好。我們預測美國市場在上半季的增長會較緩慢，但成長會一直持續到下半年。

No Time Chunks	Present Time Chunks	Past Time Chunks	Future Time Chunks
		• *acquired*	

答案 ▶

請利用下表核對答案。

No Time Chunks （不受限時間的 chunks）	Present Time Chunks （現在時間的 chunks）	Past Time Chunks （過去時間的 chunks）	Future Time Chunks （未來時間的 chunks）
• is very attractive • suggests • means • show	• has experienced • have traded • has affected • have been • have reached • is continuing • has been • is already starting • is ready for	• was regarded • was renamed • were laid off • were made • were introduced • were modernized • took place • had • began • were not	• can expect • are tipped to • is expected to • will probably be • envisage • looks set to • looks like being • estimate • will develop • begin • does not result in

　　如果你的答案和表格提供的有出入，別擔心，這是很有可能的事。你在未來時間欄中寫的答案是否特別不同？稍後在本章裡，你對此會有更多的了解。

　　在此要特別注意的是，各段落裡動詞時態聚集的方式。第一段描寫去年發生的事件，因此動詞大多為簡單過去式 (past simple)。中間兩段是關於現況的描述，因此動詞大部分是現在完成式 (present perfect) 或現在進行式 (present continuous)，加上一些「不受限」時間的動詞來說明事實和看法。最後一段描述的是未來的展望，所以用了很多未來用語。雖然這些動詞大部分是簡單現在式，但後面接的卻是未來才會發生的事件，因此我將之歸類在未來時間的用語中。寫情況概述時的組織架構最好能像這樣，以便讀者能立即看出每個段落描述的時間範圍。

　　至於不同時間範圍內發生的事件該如何描述呢？現在請繼續深入學習，我們就先從過去時間的用語開始吧。

過去時間的用語

　　情況概述中，描述過去時間的用語其實非常簡單，只要使用簡單過去式的動詞即可。唯一你會覺得有困難的地方，可能只是將某些動詞的不規則三態記起來，還有確認所使用的時間 chunks 符合動詞時態的意義。現在來看一下第一個課題。

TASK 2.3

請完成下表。

become	*became*	*become*
begin		
bring		
come		
do		
feel		
find		
get		
give		
go		
have		
hear		
hold		
keep		
know		
learn		

leave		
let		
make		
meet		
pay		
put		
read		
say		
see		
send		
set		
take		
tell		
think		
understand		
write		

答案 ▶

請利用下面的表格核對答案，並特別注意答錯的地方。

提案 必備語庫 **2.1**

become	*became*	*become*
begin	began	begun
bring	brought	brought
come	came	come
do	did	done
feel	felt	felt
find	found	found
get	got	got/gotten
give	gave	given
go	went	gone
have	had	had
hear	heard	heard
hold	held	held
keep	kept	kept
know	knew	known
learn	learned	learned

leave	left	left
let	let	let
make	made	made
meet	met	met
pay	paid	paid
put	put	put
read	read	read
say	said	said
see	saw	seen
send	sent	sent
set	set	set
take	took	taken
tell	told	told
think	thought	thought
understand	understood	understood
write	wrote	written

★ 📁 語庫小叮嚀

◆ 在英式用法中，get 的過去分詞是用 got；在美式用法中，則是用 gotten。

◆ Read 的現在式唸成 [rid]，過去式和過去分詞則是唸成 [rɛd]。

　　現在來看一看第二個課題——確定句中的時間 chunks 確實符合過去時間的意義。聽起來很簡單，但是我知道很多人常栽在這裡。

TASK 2.4

請將下列的時間 chunks 分類並填入下表中。

1. this year

2. last year

3. last quarter

4. during that time

5. during this time

6. ago

7. year-to-date

8. yesterday

9. this week

10. this quarter

11. then

12. in 1999

13. so far

Past Time Chunks	Present Time Chunks

答案

請以下列語庫核對答案。

提案 必備語庫 2.2

Past Time Chunks （過去時間 chunks）	Present Time Chunks （現在時間 chunks）
• last year • last quarter • during that time • ago • yesterday • then • in 1999	• this year • during this time • year-to-date • this week • this quarter • so far

★ 語庫小叮嚀

◆ 你應該還沒忘記吧！過去時間的 chunks 要記得與簡單過去式連用，現在時間的 chunks 則記得要與現在完成式或現在進行式連用。

◆ Year-to-date 意指從年初到撰寫提案或報告的時間，不見得是完整的一年。

　　你現在已經知道時間 chunks 和動詞時態要相符，寫出來的句子才會是對的，那麼現在就讓我們來做此類練習吧！

TASK 2.5

請閱讀下列句子，並改正句子中錯誤的動詞時態。請看範例。

1. Market share increases sharply this quarter.

Market share has increased sharply this quarter.

2. Sales went up dramatically so far.

3. The number of court cases against the company has declined slightly last year.

4. Profits went up year-to-date.

5. Advertising costs went up sharply this quarter.

6. Production costs have gone up steadily last year.

7. Budgets remained the same this year.

答案 ▶

2. Sales have gone up dramatically so far.
3. The number of court cases against the company declined slightly last year.
4. Profits have gone up year-to-date.
5. Advertising costs have gone up sharply this quarter.
6. Production costs went up steadily last year
7. Budgets have remained the same this year.

　　練習了這麼多句子，有沒有已經抓到訣竅了呢？其實只要記得一個技巧就行了，就是動詞的時態永遠要跟著時間 chunks 而改變。

　　好，如果都記得檢查動詞的不規則過去式，並確定所使用的時間 chunks 跟動詞時態是相等的，那麼描述過去發生的事件應該就沒問題了。

TASK 2.6

請回頭重新閱讀 Task 2.2 的情況概述，注意動詞時態和時間 chunks 是否吻合，特別注意描述過去時間的第一段。

延伸寫作 ▶

請寫一篇短文，描述公司從成立到去年底的發展狀況。你的公司在過去發生了哪些重大事件？

參考答案 ▶

以下提供我的參考答案。

　　My company was founded by the Chen family during the late 60s. At that time, the company specialized in man-made fibers. One of the first major contracts the company won was to supply textiles for a company who produced parachutes, tents and other equipment for the Taiwanese military. In 1974, the company moved into uniform production and began to directly supply the Taiwanese military with uniforms. During the 70s, other international military contracts followed, including South Korea and Thailand. During the early 80s, developments in new man-made fibers allowed the company to produce textiles that were light, strong and waterproof. In the early 90s, new weaving techniques helped in the development of parachutes that were twenty times lighter and stronger than previous models. When Mr. Chen Junior took over control of the company in 1998, the company started to diversify into civilian adventure gear, such as mountaineering equipment and clothes.

 W o r d   L i s t

parachutes ['pærə͵ʃut] *n.* 降落傘

civilain [sɪ`vɪljən] *adj.* 民用的

gear [gɪr] *n.*（供某種用途的）工具／裝備／衣服

【內容摘要】

　　公司在六○年代末期由陳氏家族所成立，那時專門製造人造纖維。第一個大合約是供應布料給一家生產降落傘等軍用品的公司，1974 年起，公司進而生產制服，在七○年代，從南韓跟泰國等國際軍方合約接踵而至。八○年代起，更生產了輕盈、強韌、防水的布料。到了九○年代，新的紡織技術更將降落傘的製造推向另一高峰。在1998 年，陳家第二代接管公司後，公司便開始多元化發展的時代。

　　別忘了運用在上面學習到的知識，並特別注意時態和時間 chunks 是否使用正確。

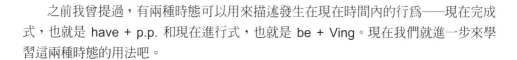
現在時間的用語

之前我曾提過，有兩種時態可以用來描述發生在現在時間內的行為——現在完成式，也就是 have + p.p. 和現在進行式，也就是 be + Ving。現在我們就進一步來學習這兩種時態的用法吧。

TASK 2.7

請看下面的表格，研讀這兩種時態的涵義。

	意義	範例	註解
現在進行式	• 仍在進行中、尚未有結果的行為。	• We <u>are still waiting</u> for the sales results for last quarter. • I <u>am currently working</u> on a report for the shareholders.	• 行為和時間都尚未完成→我們正在等。 • 行為和時間都尚未完成→報告還沒寫好。
現在完成式	• 現今存在的、已經完成的行為。	• I <u>have just completed</u> the report. • We <u>have managed</u> to increase our market share by 13% in the second half year.	• 行為已完成，但是時間範圍還未結束→報告現在存在。 • 上半年還沒結束，但已獲得結果→13%。

這裡需要記得的重點是，每個動詞都提供了時間和行為的資訊。這兩種時態的共通點是時間都是未完成的，行為則不一定，有可能是尚未完成（現在進行式），亦可能是已經完成（現在完成式）。

請做下面的 Task，確定已完全瞭解此一概念。接著我們會更進一步探討各時態的用法。

TASK 2.8

請閱讀下面的短文，將所有現在式的動詞畫線。這些動詞指的是一個進行中的行為，

還是指行為的結果？請完成表格。

【背景說明】

　　Pharmax 有限公司是一家位於德國的跨國藥商，有一款人氣新藥原本計畫在台灣市場銷售，卻因當地政府的諸多規定而暫緩推出。以下是新藥行銷提案中的一小段文章。

> The company is still waiting for the results of an inquiry commissioned by the government into the effects of the new drug. Our contact in the department has informed us that the report has been written, but hasn't yet been approved. There is a backlog of work, since the new systems which have recently been installed in the department are not working properly. A lot of reports are being delayed because of this, not only ours, and a lot of our competitors are facing the same problem.

【提案摘要】

　　公司正在等政府對新藥的調查結果，有消息指調查出報告已經完成，但仍未被證實。這是因為該審查部門的新系統運作不順利，因此積壓了很多工作。

Action Still in Progress	Result of an Action

答案 ▶

請利用下表核對答案。

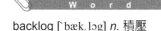

backlog [ˋbækˌlɔg] *n.* 積壓

Action Still in Progress (進行中的行為)	Result of an Action (行為的結果)
• is still waiting for	• has informed us
• are not working	• has been written
• are being delayed	• hasn't yet been approved
• are facing	• have recently been installed

　　你注意到了嗎？寫提案或報告時，實際上有些動詞會比較常以某個時態出現，某些時間 chunks 也總是跟某種時態一起用。

提案 必備語庫 **2.3**

請研讀下表以及語庫小叮嚀。

	常用動詞	時間 chunks
現在進行式	• wait • hope • try • work • change	• currently • still • these days
現在完成式	• change • complete • become • ask • achieve • decide • develop • finish • find • improve • happen • receive • send • speak • write	• since • for • yet • already • recently • ever • just • so far • lately • these days • never ... before

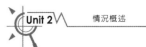

★ 語庫小叮嚀

◆ Since 用來描述某個時間點;for 則用來描述某段時期;yet 僅用在否定句和問句中;ever 也僅用在問句、否定句和條件子句中;lately 通常用在問句中。

◆ 記住,這些動詞不是每次都用同種時態,只是比較常用而已。下筆前,務必想清楚自己想表達的意思,再來決定該使用哪一種時態。

◆ 就如同我之前提過的,時間 chunks 務必和正確的時態一起搭配使用。如果搭配錯誤,讀者會一頭霧水,不解其意。

TASK 2.9

現在,就讓我們利用上述學到的知識來做一個 Task 吧!閱讀下列句子,並從語庫 2.3 中選出最適當的時間 chunks 填入空格裡。

1. We've been in this market _____ many years.
2. There has been a steady decline in profits _____ the Asian financial crisis.
3. We've _____ been in merger talks with one of our main competitors.
4. We've _____ met our targets for this year.
5. Has this market _____ been profitable for you?
6. We have _____ merged with our competitor.
7. We have seen a big increase in bankruptcies _____ .
8. We have _____ seen such rapid growth in this market _____ .
9. We are _____ working on a new billing system.
10. Have you finished that report _____ .
11. We are _____ waiting to receive the go-ahead on this.
12. There have been many new developments in the market _____ .

答案 ▶

答案以黑體字表示。

1. We've been in this market **for** many years.
2. There has been a steady decline in profits **since** the Asian financial crisis.
3. We've **just/recently** been in merger talks with one of our main competitors.
4. We've **already/never** met our targets for this year.
5. Has this market **ever** been profitable for you?
6. We have **just/recently/never** merged with our competitor.
7. We have seen a big increase in bankruptcies these **days/so far/since**.
8. We have **never** seen such rapid growth in this market **before/since**.
9. We are **currently/already** working on a new billing system.
10. Have you finished that report **yet**?
11. We are **still** waiting to receive the go-ahead on this.
12. There have been many new developments in the market **these days/recently/since**.

TASK 2.10

請閱讀某份情況概述中的一段短文，並從語庫 2.3 中選出適當的動詞，以正確時態填入空格中。有些空格也需填入一些時間 chunks。

【背景說明】

　　Go Far 公司是一間台灣的旅行社，他們近來展開了一項專案，預計將所有服務網路化，不過卻因為市場上缺乏擁有此類技術的工程師而被迫延後。營運經理靈機一動，想到解決問題的辦法。以下是他提案中的情況概述。

> There ___(1)___ a lot of new developments recently. We ___(2)___ our billing system to an automatic online registration. We

_____(3)_____ that this will cut costs. The first phase of this project _____(4)_____, and already we _____(5)_____ that customers like it. As a result, our customer relations _____(6)_____. While we _____(7)_____ the whole project, we _____(8)_____ hard to achieve completion by the end of the year. It _____(9)_____ more difficult recently to recruit good computer programmers in this market, and this is affecting the progress of the project. We _____(10)_____ to recruit some overseas programmers, but there are issues with the Department of Labour regarding work permits. The CEO _____(11)_____ to the Minister and _____(12)_____ his contacts in the government to help, but we _____(13)_____ for a reply.

Some key customers _____(14)_____ for discounts for bulk orders, and we _____(15)_____ to grant them this. We _____(16)_____ good relations with these customers, and we _____(17)_____ to them informally about the possibility of them paying for their orders in advance.

答案 ▶

1. have been
2. are changing
3. are hoping
4. has just been completed
5. have found
6. have improved
7. have not yet finished
8. are working
9. has become
10. are trying
11. has written
12. has asked
13. are still waiting

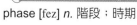

W o r d   L i s t

phase [fez] *n.* 階段；時期   grant [ɡrænt] *v.* 允諾；答應
recruit [rɪˈkrut] *v.* 招募

14. have recently asked
15. have decided
16. have developed
17. have sopken

延伸寫作 ▶

請寫一篇短文描述公司這半年來的現況。請敘述產業界和市場上現在的趨勢,以及你這半年來已經達成的目標。

參考答案 ▶

> This half year has been difficult overall for the travel industry in Taiwan. Terrorist fears abroad, and the low Taiwan dollar have resulted in more people staying at home. Despite this overall decline, the number of travelers going to the US and Canada is declining, compared with last year, while the number of people going to Europe is going up, also compared with last year. The number of people going to Asian countries has stayed more or less the same. These days the number of people choosing to travel independently is also increasing, and this is affecting the size of tour groups, which are generally getting smaller. We are currently thinking about how to meet the needs of independent travelers to take advantage of this growing sector.

【內容摘要】
　　台灣的旅遊業在今年上半普遍表現不佳。跟去年相比,到美國及加拿大的旅客有些微的下降,反之,到歐洲的旅客卻增加了,到亞洲的旅客則大致相同,自助旅行者的增加也讓跟團的人變的越來越少,我們最近也在思考如何符合此類客戶的需求。

未來時間的用語

　　英文裡的未來時間用語常叫人恨得牙癢癢的，因為對未來不同的層面得用不同的未來 chunks 表達，沒辦法全部都套用同一種。因此，決定該用哪一種未來 chunks 的最佳起點，就是先思考要寫的是 personal 未來，還是 impersonal 未來。所謂 personal 未來，指的是個人的未來計畫和安排，以及其他和自己有關的未來人事物，包括家人、朋友、商業夥伴、同事或其他對自己生活有直接關連的人。而 impersonal 未來則泛指世上的未來事件，如經濟、環境、國際政治舞台、你的商業領域、你公司銷售產品和服務的市場等。

　　一旦決定好要寫的是 personal 還是 impersonal 的未來之後，接下來就需要思考這個未來事件是確定還是不確定的。兩者都設想周全後，就只要選擇最適當的時間 chunks 或動詞時態來表達即可。

TASK 2.11

　　請研讀下面的圖示。

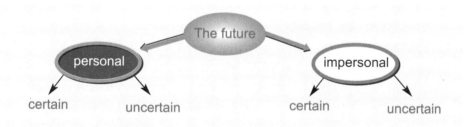

　　在這章節裡，我打算專注在 impersonal 未來的用法，因為情況概述中最需要描述的就是這種用法。至於 personal 未來，我會在第六章中教你。現在我們就先從 impersonal 的確定未來著手吧。

　　要表示 impersonal 的確定未來事件時，有兩種 chunks — will V 和 be going to V。兩者表達的意思一樣，但 be going to V 可強調你有證據說明你對未來的看法是確定的，而 will V 則僅僅是在陳述某件 impersonal 的確定未來而已。

TASK 2.12

請閱讀下面的情況概述,將所有未來式畫底線。請注意這些詞的用法,並想想他們所代表的意義。

【背景說明】

　　EPF 公司是一家在中國大陸、台灣、香港有多家分行的中國銀行子公司,專門貸款給想買車的人。下面是該公司的信貸部經理在中國加入世界貿易組織 (WTO) 之前寫的情況概述。

> 　　China's entry into the WTO is going to mean lower tariffs on all the parts, tools, and equipment that manufacturers need to build their cars. However, these reductions will be gradual, so their impact on retail prices will not be immediate. Competition, meanwhile, is building. In addition to GM's Buick series, the Honda Accord, the Audi A6, and the VW Passat are currently trying to enter China's luxury car market.
>
> 　　In the high-volume compact car segment, GM's Snail is going to sell at US$6,700 compared with US$11,000 for the Daihatsu Charade, and US$7,200 for the Suzuki Alto. And while the WTO is going to make imports cheaper, it will also benefit finished car importers, who, by 2006, will only pay a 20% duty compared with today's 35%. Further, the WTO will do nothing about allowing foreign companies or banks to provide consumer financing to the consumer market. Only Chinese banks will be able to provide car financing and, due to the lack of a credit tracking system among banks, only 15% of the 600,000 cars sold in China last year were financed this way. The opportunity for growth is clear.

 Word List

tariff [ˋtærɪf] *n.* 關稅;稅率
GM (General Motors) 美國通用汽車公司
VW (Volkswagen) 福斯汽車

compact [kəmˋpækt] *adj.* (汽車) 小型的
segment [ˋsɛgmənt] *n.* 部分;部門
Daihatsu 大發汽車

【內容摘要】

中國加入 WTO 之後，意味著汽車製造商將可取得較低關稅的汽車零組件。不過降低關稅會是緩慢的，因此零售價也不可能立即降得太多。除了 GM 的 Buick 系列外，Honda 的 Accord，Audi 的 A6 和 VW 的 Passat 也都積極地要進入中國的頂級車市場。

在小型車部分，GM 的 Snail 車款的售價也比 Daihastu 的 Charade 以及 Suzuki 的 Alto 來得便宜，雖然 WTO 的宗旨是讓進口品變得更便宜，不過也會讓終端的汽車進口商獲利，因為到了 2006 年，他們只需付 20% 的稅率。此外，WTO 對消費信貸將採取放任的態度，僅有中國的銀行可以提供車子的信貸，不過中國也只有 15% 的車子是採取此種貸款，因此成長的機會很大。

答案▶

相信挑出這些未來式動詞並不難，對吧？為了加強你對 will V 以及 be going to V 的認知，請看以下例子。

1. China's entry into the WTO is going to mean lower tariffs.
作者選擇使用 be going to V，是因為他希望用其他加入 WTO 的國家等先例當證據，證明 WTO 的成立宗旨就是降低關稅，而事實也的確是如此。

2. However, these reductions will be gradual, so their impact on retail prices will not be immediate.
作者選擇使用 will V，是因為他不認為有必要強調證據，或者因為他沒有任何證據。

不管你使用的是哪一種未來式，一切都只是選擇性的問題而已——選擇你想傳達的意思，並使用可傳達這個意思的用語。這些問題的答案沒有對錯之分。記住，文法的意義就在於選擇。重點在於你能否確實掌握每個字串的意思，並運用得宜。

好了，對 impersonal 確定未來用法的學習到此告一段落。讓我們來研究 impersonal 的不確定未來用語，也就是所謂的預測用語。

TASK 2.13

請研讀下列語庫。

提案 必備語庫 2.4 ▶

• … n.p. … prospects are fairly limited.	• It looks as though + n. clause …
• … envisage n.p. …	• There's every/little chance that + n. clause …
• … be tipped to V …	• It looks like + n. clause …
• … analysts predict that + n. clause …	• It is highly probable that + n. clause …
• … look set to V …	• The indications are that + n. clause …
• There's every/little chance of n.p. …	• … be due to V …
• There's every/little chance of Ving …	• The outlook is adj. …
• It is unlikely that + n. clause ...	• … in the short term …
• It looks like being n.p.	• … in the long term …
• … be expected to V …	• … in the medium term …
• … envisage that + n. clause. …	• … prospects (for sth.) are looking good/bad …
• … will probably V …	• … might V …

TASK 2.14

現在請利用上列語庫找出下面的句子的錯誤，並寫上正確答案。請見範例。

1. Employment prospects are looking like good in the long term.
  Employment prospects are looking good in the long term.

2. There's little chance that a promotion in the short term.

3. The board look sets to ask for his resignation.

4. We have envisaged an economic downturn next year.

5. The indications are that there's increased competition next year.

6. It looks as the company might go bankrupt.

7. He is tipped taking the job.

_____

8. Economic prospects are fairly limiting.

_____

9. The market is expecting to grow by 20%.

_____

10. It is unlikely that the market are improving.

_____

11. It is highly probable that downsizing are taking place.

_____

答案 ▶

請核對你答案。

2. There's little chance of a promotion in the short term.
3. The board looks set to ask for his resignation.
4. We envisage an economic downturn next year.
5. The indications are that there'll be increased competition next year.
6. It looks as though the company might go bankrupt.
7. He is tipped to take the job.
8. Economic prospects are fairly limited.
9. The market is expected to grow by 20%.
10. It is unlikely that the market will improve.
11. It is highly probable that downsizing will take place.

　　許多以 n. clause 結尾的 set-phrases 後面都會接 ... will V ...。

TASK 2.15

請閱讀下面情況概述，在已經學過的預測字串下畫底線。並注意他們的用法。

【背景說明】

　　MIT 是一家石油化學製造公司，不論台灣或中國都設有工廠。這份情況概述出自一份提案，目標是刪減原料儲存量、節省存貨成本。寫作時間在波斯灣戰爭之前。

　　The indications are that the price of oil, which ended in 1999 at more than US$25 a barrel, will lower—but only to around US$20 a barrel next year. Natural gas prices look set to rise to US$2.50 per thousand cubic feet. Strong economies in the United States and Europe are expected to keep prices up. Analysts predict that OPEC will increase its production to help keep prices moderate. We envisage that Iraq will be encouraged to produce and sell more oil on world markets. However, there's little chance that there will be a change in Saddam Hussein's behavior or hold on power, a factor that will ultimately affect supply and price.

【內容摘要】

　　有徵象指出原油的價格明年（2000 年）將會降到一桶 20 美元左右，天然瓦斯的價格則會攀升，美國和歐洲強勁的經濟會讓石油價格更高，但分析家預測 OPEC 會增加產量讓價格持平在一定的水準。我們預測伊拉克會增加產能，不過海珊有可能繼續執政，因此供給和售價還是有可能會受到影響。

答案

請以語庫 2.4 核對答案。

延伸寫作

請寫出一篇短文，概述你對自己的產業、市場和商機在下一年的預測。

參考答案

以下是針對製藥業所寫的情況預測。

> The outlook for the pharmaceutical industry in Taiwan for the next year is pretty much the same as this year. No great changes to government regulations are expected, and the numbers of patients for the different drugs are not expected to change that much either. In our market, the market share of our main product looks set to increase, as doctors and patients become more aware of the benefits of the drug. However, our main competitors are tipped to increase spending on marketing their main drug, which means that we might have to increase our spending as well. In my company, the indications are that there'll be no pay raise next year.

【內容摘要】

　　台灣製藥業明年的前景還是會跟今年差不多，政府法規跟病人對不同藥的需求都不會有太大的改變，主力產品的市佔率預期會增加，由於對手可能會增加行銷預算，所以我們也應跟進。此外，就公司內部的情況而言，明年要加薪似乎是不太可能了。

　　寫關於未來事件時，別忘了一樣得特別注意 MWIs 是否使用正確。

　　本章到此告一段落，可以繼續學習下一章了。但別急，先回到引言的學習清單，確定所有項目都已確實理解了。

 W o r d　L i s t

pharmaceutical [ˌfɑrməˋsutɪk] *adj.* 製藥的；藥學的

Unit 3

提出建議

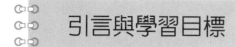 引言與學習目標

　　提案的核心在於提出建議的段落。而這也是你提出改變或建議的地方，因此語言的精準度非常重要，如此一來，讀者才能將注意力集中在你計畫的品質上，不因你的用語而分心。

　　在本章裡，你將學會說明計畫的用語。

　　本章結束時，各位應達成的「學習目標」如下：

> ❑ 有能力使用建議的 verb chunks 。
> ❑ 有能力使用建議的 set-phrases。
> ❑ 有能力寫出不同程度的正式或非正式建議。
> ❑ 研讀過一名管理顧問寫的外部提案。
> ❑ 研讀過公司經理寫的內部提案。

建議的 verb chunks

TASK 3.1

請閱讀下面的提案並回答問題。

【背景說明】

　　近來布宜斯進口公司和高雄分公司間出現一些問題。成本持續穩定的增長，銷售收益卻直直滑落，分公司和母公司之間的溝通又很少。股東的不滿隨之而來，台北的母公司因此派了一名資深經理南下高雄進行調查。以下是該名經理調查後的提案。

　　　Having spent some time in the Southern branch and having interviewed all the managers there, I would like to make the following preliminary proposals.

　　　It is recommended that the branch manager submit weekly operational reports to head office. These reports should provide information about weekly income and expenditures. This will give head office greater control over weekly budgets and allow us to better oversee operations. I also suggest that yearly budgets from all project owners in the branch be submitted and approved by head office at the start of each financial year.

　　　Regarding the current staffing levels, my recommendation here is that at least one member of staff be laid off. This would help to keep costs down. There also ought to be stricter controls regarding the hiring of temp staff, which is happening too frequently.

 W o r d   L i s t

preliminary [prɪˋlɪməˌnɛrɪ] *adj.*
初步的；序言(性)的
submitt [səbˋmɪt] *v.* 提交；呈遞

expenditure [ɪkˋspɛndɪtʃə] *n.* 支出額；經費
temp [tɛmp] *n.* 臨時雇員（尤指臨時祕書）

It is also proposed that the branch manager be replaced with someone of greater experience, preferably from head office.

I propose to conduct a follow-up report in two months to assess the result of these recommendations. However, it is strongly recommended that these steps be implemented at once, before the situation in the Southern branch gets out of hand.

【提案摘要】

在訪談了一些經理之後，該名資深經理提出了一些建議。1. 分行經理應每週向母公司提出營運報告。2. 在每年的財會年度開始時，分行的專案領導人能提出年度預算。3. 針對目前的人事政策，他也建議應裁減些員工。4. 對聘請臨時雇員應有更嚴厲的控管。5. 他也提議母公司最好能派遣較資深的人來任職分行經理。6. 在兩個月內進行一項追蹤報告，評估成果。7. 在情況尚未惡化到極點之前，能立刻執行。

該名經理提出哪些改善的建議？請列在下面的空格中。請看範例。

1. *weekly operational reports* _____
2. _____
3. _____
4. _____
5. _____

答案 ▶

2. yearly budgets from all project owners
3. one member of staff laid off
4. stricter controls regarding temp staff
5. branch manager be replaced

implement ［ˈɪmplə͵mɛnt］ v. 履行；實施

　　除了這些特定建議之外，該名經理也先用一個整體性的建議來引導出其他建議，最後提出應儘速處理的計畫，以及應趕緊做出的改變。

　　現在我們來看一看提案中使用的語言。提案中有兩種語言項目：較短的 verb chunks 和較長的 set-phrases。我們先來看一看 verb chunks。

TASK 3.2

請將這些 verb chunks 分類。請決定有幾個類別，每個類別又是什麼。

提案 必備語庫 3.1 ▶

• … recommend that + n. clause …	• … should not V …
• … recommend n.p. …	• … ought to V …
• … propose that + n. clause …	• … suggest that + n. clause …
• … propose n.p. …	• … propose to V …
• … propose Ving …	• … should V …
• … ought not to V …	• … recommend Ving …
• … suggest n.p. …	• … suggest Ving …

答案 ▶

Verb chunks 的分類方式很多。你可能會根據動詞、或者以 n.p. 結尾的 chunks 、that + clause 或 Ving 等方式來做分類。不管你的分類方式為何，希望透過這個練習，你會更加注意 verb chunks 之間相似和相異的模式。

> ★ 📁 語庫小叮嚀
>
> ◆ Suggest 是這三個動詞中最不正式的一個，propose 則最正式，不過你不需太擔心這兩者間的差別，因為差別微乎其微。
> ◆ Suggest、recommend 和 propose 的模式一樣，得和 that + n. clause 或 n.p. 或 Ving 一起用。
> ◆ 在 suggest that + n. clause、recommend that + n. clause 和 propose that + n. clause 三個 chunks 後面的動詞記得要用原型，也就是完全不要管時態或第三人稱；不要加上 -ed、-s ，也無須在前面加上 should 或 ought to 。

◆ 使用建議型態的 chunks 時，that 可以省略，但建議你還是使用會比較好，以免出錯。
◆ Propose 後面可用 to V，意思等同於 plan to V 或 intend to V，但 suggest 和 recommend 後則不可接 to V。
◆ Should V 和 ought to V 的意思一樣。

TASK 3.3

請回到 Task 3.1，找出所有研讀過的 verb chunks，並畫底線，請注意這些 verb chunks 的用法。

答案 ▶

Having spent some time in the Southern branch and having interviewed all the managers there, I would like to make the following preliminary proposals.

It is recommended that the branch manager submit weekly operational reports to head office. These reports should provide information about weekly income and expenditures. This will give head office greater control over weekly budgets and allow us to better oversee operations. I also suggest that yearly budgets from all project owners in the branch be submitted and approved by head office at the start of each financial year.

Regarding the current staffing levels, my recommendation here is that at least one member of staff be laid off. This would help to keep costs down. There also ought to be stricter controls regarding the hiring of temp staff, which is happening too frequently.

It is also proposed that the branch manager be replaced with someone of greater experience, preferably from head office.

I propose to conduct a follow-up report in two months to assess the result of these recommendations. However, it is strongly recommended that these steps be implemented at once, before the situation in the Southern branch gets out of hand.

TASK 3.4

好，我們現在就來練習使用這些不同的 chunks，如此一來，你就可以知道如何使用它們了。

請研讀下列句子，看得出來其中的模式嗎？

1. I suggest that you implement the plan as soon as possible.
I suggest implementing the plan as soon as possible.
I suggest a quick implementation.

2. I recommend that you increase prices by 2%.
I recommend increasing prices by 2%.
I recommend a 2% price increase.

3. I propose that you change suppliers.
I propose changing suppliers.
I propose a supplier change.

答案 ▶

希望你看得出來將 n. clause 轉換成 Ving 的方法，以及將 Ving 轉換成 word partner-ships 的方法。

若提案的對象不是自己的 team 時，你可以使用 I suggest/propose/recommend that **you** ...；若提案的對象是自己的 team 時，則可使用 I suggest/propose/recom-mend that **we** ... 或者就直接使用 I suggest/propose/recommend Ving ... 即可。

TASK 3.5

現在請用上述所教的兩種轉換方式重新改寫以下各句，請見範例。

1. I propose that we increase the marketing budget.

I propose increasing the marketing budget.

I propose a marketing budget increase.

2. I recommend that we develop a new product range.

_____

_____

3. I suggest that we employ three more full-time engineers.

_____

_____

4. I propose doing some market research.

_____

_____

5. I recommend changing the **specs**.

_____

_____

6. I suggest buying a new machine.

_____

_____

7. I propose an immediate start.

_____

_____

8. I suggest a delayed start.

_____

_____

W o r d　L i s t

specs [spɛks] *pl. n.* 規格

9. I recommend cancellation.

_____

_____

答案 ▶

請核對你的答案。

2. I recommend developing a new product range.
I recommend a new product range development.

3. I suggest employing three more full-time engineers.
I suggest three more full-time engineers.

4. I propose some market research.
Ipropose that we do some market research.

5. I recommend a specs change.
I recommend that we change the specs.

6. I suggest a new machine.
I suggest that we buy a new machine.

7. I propose that we start immediately.
I propose starting immediately.

8. I suggest that we delay the start.
I suggest delaying the start.

9. I recommend canceling.
I recommend that we cancel.

TASK 3.6

請看以下句子。如果覺得某個句子有錯，請予以改正。如果覺得某個句子正確無誤，就寫上 correct（正確的），有些句子的答案不只一個。請見範例。

1. I suggest you to raise prices.	*I suggest that you raise prices.*
2. I recommend a new approach.	
3. I propose to implement this strategy next quarter.	
4. I recommend that you should close this branch.	
5. I suggest that we invest in new equipment.	
6. I recommend to go on with the project.	
7. I suggest a price increase.	
8. I propose that we should call a meeting.	
9. I propose that we try to reduce costs.	
10. I suggest you to try harder.	
11. I suggest that we should con-tact them.	
12. I propose you to discuss this with the client.	

W o r d L i s t

call [kɔl] v. 召開（會議）

答案 ▶

請以下表核對你的答案。

2. I recommend a new approach.	Correct
3. I propose to implement this strategy next quarter.	Correct
4. I recommend that you should close this branch.	I recommend that you close this branch.
5. I suggest that we invest in new equipment.	Correct
6. I recommend to go on with the project.	I recommend going on with the project.
7. I suggest a price increase.	Correct
8. I propose that we should call a meeting.	I propose that we call a meeting.
9. I propose that we try to reduce costs.	Correct
10. I suggest you to try harder.	I suggest that you try harder.
11. I suggest that we should contact them.	I suggest that we contact them.
12. I propose you to discuss this with the client.	I propose that you discuss this with the client.

現在你已很會使用 verb chunks 了，我們接著就來研讀建議的 set-phrases 吧。

建議的 set-phrases

TASK 3.7

請將下列的 set-phrases 分門別類，類別的多寡和種類由你決定。

提案 必備語庫 3.2 ▶

- I would like to make the following proposal(s).
- It is recommended that + n.clause …
- My suggestion here is to V …
- I would like to make the following recommendation(s).
- My recommendation here is that + n. clause …
- It is proposed that + n.clause …
- My proposal here is to V …
- My proposal here is for n.p. …

- My recommendation here is for n.p. …
- It is suggested that + n. clause …
- My suggestion here is that + n. clause …
- I would like to make the following suggestion(s).
- My proposal here is that + n. clause …
- My recommendation here is to V …
- My suggestion here is for n.p. …

答案 ▶

上述 set-phrases 的分類方法有很多種。你可依據主要動詞或主要名詞末分類，以 It … 或 My … 開頭，或者是依據每個 set-phrase 結尾的模式來分類。不管你如何分類這些 set-phrases，希望透過這個練習，你對它們之間相似或相異的模式會更加敏銳。

★ 📁 語庫小叮嚀

◆ 一般說來，若是要寫較正式和較長的提案，請使用語庫 3.2 中的 set-phrases；若是要寫較不正式和較短的提案，請使用語庫 3.1 中的 verb chunks。不過在同一份文件中，set-phrases 和 verb chunks 均可使用，以提高寫作變化。

◆ 如果想要正式一些，並在你和你的建議之間製造一種距離，可使用以 It is … 開頭的 set-phrases。

T A S K 3.8

請回到 Task 3.1，找出所有研讀過的建議 set-phrases，並畫底線，請注意這些 set-phrases 的用法。

答案 ▶

> Having spent some time in the Southern branch and having interviewed all the managers there, <u>I would like to make the following preliminary proposals</u>.
>
> <u>It is recommended that</u> the branch manager submit weekly operational reports to head office. These reports should provide information about weekly income and expenditures. This will give head office greater control over weekly budgets and allow us to better oversee operations. I also suggest that yearly budgets from all project owners in the branch be submitted and approved by head office at the start of each financial year.
>
> Regarding the current staffing levels, <u>my recommendation here is that</u> at least one member of staff be laid off. This would help to keep costs down. There also ought to be stricter controls regarding the hiring of temp staff, which is happening too frequently.
>
> It is also proposed that the branch manager be replaced with someone of greater experience, preferably from head office.
>
> I propose to conduct a follow-up report in two months to assess the result of these recommendations. However, it is strongly recommended that these steps be implemented at once, before the situation in the Southern branch gets out of hand.

　　還記得我在前言中提到的 set-phrases 用法嗎？請做下面的 Task，來幫助你提高對短字、詞尾、還有 set-phrases 結尾的敏銳度，確定你對 set-phrases 的概念是正確無誤的。

TASK 3.9

請改正下列句子中的 set-phrases。每個句子的正確答案不只一個。請看範例。

1. I would like make the following proposals.

I would like to make the following proposals.

2. It is recommend that we increase the unit price.

3. It is suggested to adjust the pricing controls.

4. Our recommendations here is to reduce the budget.

5. We would like to make the following recommend.

6. Our proposal here is that go over the specs.

答案 ▶

請核對你的答案。

2. It is recommended that we increase the unit price.
3. It is suggested that we adjust the pricing controls.
4. Our recommendation here is to reduce the budget.
5. We would like to make the following recommendations.
6. Our proposal here is that we go over the specs.

　　好，現在我們來試寫幾個簡單的提議。在下面的 Task 當中，請決定這個情況應使用非正式的 verb chunks 還是正式的 set-phrases。

TASK 3.10

請閱讀以下的情況和指示，然後寫出一個建議句。請見範例。

1. 你辦公室裡的影印機老是壞掉，請建議購置一台新的。

   I suggest that we buy a new one.

2. 你辦公室裡的咖啡機老是壞掉，請建議購買一台新的。

3. 你的辦公室太小，請建議換間較大的辦公室。

3. 你的團隊無法承擔工作量，請建議雇用一名兼職的臨時員工。

4. 你目前進行的專案速度比想像中的慢，請建議延後期限。

5. 你的利潤越來越少，請建議一條新的產品線。

6. 你競爭對手的市場佔有率越來越高，請建議擴展海外業務。

7. 你對目前的廣告策略不滿意，請建議換一家廣告公司。

8. 你老闆的生日到了，請提議開生日派對。

9. 你的供應商索價過高，請建議換一家供應商。

答案▶

你可以用下列的建議答案核對自己的答案。倘若你的答案相差甚遠，請檢查其中所有的 set-phrases 和 verb chunks 是正確無誤的。

2. I suggest buying a new one.
3. I suggest that we move to a larger office.
3. I recommend that we hire a part-time temp.
4. My proposal here is that we extend the project deadline.

5. It is proposed that we introduce a new product line.

6. It is proposed that we expand overseas.

7. My proposal here is for an agency change.

8. We should have a party for him.

9. My recommendation is that we change suppliers.

　　為進一步練習使用這種用語，建議你用 set-phrases、verb chunks 互換的方式，改寫你為這個 Task 所寫下的句子。舉個例子，如果你在第二題中寫的是 I suggest buying a new one.，可把這一句改成 My suggestion is that we buy a new one.，這種改寫語言項目的練習做得越多，你對語言項目越能運用自如，而相對地，你在提案中正確使用這些句子的自信也就會越高。

　　最後，我們再來看一個提案範例。Task 3.1 中的提案是公司內部的人所寫的，因此所有的主詞都用 I 或 we。下面要閱讀的提案則是出自一名管理顧問之手，因此使用的主詞不同。閱讀時請留意這個差別。此外也請特別注意在本章中學過的字串。

TASK 3.11

請閱讀下列提案，鞏固在本章中學過的技巧。

【背景說明】

　　康福製藥公司是一間位於台北的中型公司。雖然近來公司的營收不錯，士氣卻很低瀰，員工離職率很高。辦公室經理僱用了一名環境顧問來找出提高士氣和留住員工的辦法。以下是該名顧問的提案。

　　Having spent a week in your office observing your staff going about the course of their daily duties, we would like to make the following preliminary proposals.

　　It is recommended that the cubicle height be lowered by five inches. Your staff should be able to see over the top of their partitions

cubicle [ˈkjubɪk]] *n.* 小隔間　　　　　　partition [pɑrˈtɪʃən] *n.* 分隔間

when seated. This will facilitate management in checking that their teams are working efficiently.

We also suggest that your staff be allowed to personalize their cubicles with family photos and such personal objects. Obviously, the cubicles should not be so cluttered as to interfere with the work, but from our experience, a degree of personalized office space improves moral and productivity.

Regarding the quality of the light, our recommendation here is that you change the neon strip lighting currently in use to a warmer and softer style of lighting. There also ought to be shades in front of the windows so that those workers currently sitting in direct afternoon sunlight can see their monitors. It is also proposed that some greenery be included in your office environment: having plants in the office often improves the air quality, and hence productivity.

We propose to conduct a follow-up visit to assess the effectiveness of our suggestions sometime in the next three months. However, we strongly recommend that these changes be carried out as soon as possible so that your business can start to function more effectively.

【提案摘要】

在觀察員工執行業務的情況後，該名環境顧問提出了幾點建議。1. 建議桌子的隔間高度降低五英吋。2. 員工可用些家庭照片或個人物品將隔間個人化一些。3. 至於照明的品質，建議將霓虹燈管換成較溫暖柔和的燈光。4. 坐在窗前的員工應有些遮陽板之類的東西，以免午後的陽光刺眼，看不清螢幕。5. 建議綠化辦公室環境，例如在辦公室放些盆栽改善空氣品質。6. 在接下來的三個月內應找時間進行追蹤訪談，以評估成果。7. 能立即執行，讓公司能再次有效率地運作。

W o r d   L i s t

clutter [`klʌtə] v. 使凌亂；亂堆在

延伸寫作 ▌▶

1. 請寫一個便條給辦公室經理，提出改善辦公室的建議。
2. 請寫一份提案給老闆，提議改善目前自己工作中某些沒效率之處。

參考答案 ▌▶

以下提供我的參考答案，閱讀的同時，請用不同顏色的筆分別將學過的 verb chunks 和 set-phrases 畫底線。

Office Environment Memo

I think the office environment is hurting our productivity. The office is too dark, the kitchen area has ants, and the air quality is not good. I have three main recommendations to make. First, I recommend that we replace the glass in the windows with clear glass. Second, I suggest organizing a cleaning schedule for the kitchen area — a different department could be responsible for cleaning it each Friday. Finally, we should install air conditioning.

【提案摘要】
　　針對辦公室太暗、廚房髒亂和空氣品質不好等有害生產力的問題，有三個建議。
1. 將窗戶的玻璃換成透明玻璃。2. 排清掃班表維持廚房的整潔。3. 裝置空調。

Line Management: A Proposal

I feel that the management of my position is not clear, so I would like to make the following recommendations. Currently for overseas business, I report to our regional office, and for domestic business I report to our Taipei Sales Director only, while for everyday business activities, I report to the Kaohsiung Office Manager. My proposal here is that I report directly for all business to the Taipei Sales Director, as

---

 W o r d   L i s t

domestic [dəˈmɛstɪk] *adj.* 國內的

most of my work is domestic. If I have international business to conduct, I suggest that I report this to the Taipei Sales Director as well, who can then pass my reports up to the regional office.

【提案摘要】

由於覺得目前此職位的管理不清楚，因為針對不同的業務須向不同的主管提出報告，因此提出了直接向台北的業務主管提報業務的建議。

你的答案可能會和參考答案有些出入，但是希望至少你的 set-phrases 沒有用錯。

好了，本章到此結束。在繼續下一章之前，請回到前面的學習清單，將所有確認已經理解的項目打勾。

 W o r d   L i s t

conduct ['kɑndʌkt] v. 處理（業務）

Unit 4

評估

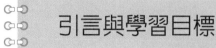

引言與學習目標

　　一旦在提案中提出計畫之後，接下來就應該評估計畫可能帶來的影響和結果。這是最需要說服力的部分，也是語言的素質和思維模式最需被彰顯的部分。正如我在第一章所提過的，評估的章節中應該放進 SWOT 分析、計畫時間表和成本效益分析，並指出執行計畫時會動員到的人員。這些內容可以用圖表有效地呈現，因此，本章的重點字串有三：一‧描述計畫目的和預期結果的字串；二‧描述假設狀況及其結果的字串；三‧以及評估計畫正反面的對比字串。

　　研讀完本章，你應達成的學習目標如下：

　　　　　❏ 有能力描述計畫的目的和結果。
　　　　　❏ 有能力描述計畫的假設狀況為何。
　　　　　❏ 有能力描述計畫假設情況下的結果。
　　　　　❏ 有能力利用對比字串，評估正反面效果 。

描述目的和預期的結果

在本章開始前，請花一點時間思考這三者之間的差別：行為的**原因**、行為的**目的**和行為的**結果**。在此，我們需要發揮哲學思考的能力，因為在英語裡，這三者可用不同的 chunks 區別出來，寫提案時務必清楚了解每一類 chunks 的確切意涵，如此才能真正傳遞你想表達的意思。

TASK 4.1

行為的目的、行為的原因和行為的結果有何差別？請想一想，如有必要可做筆記。

答案▶

我們來看一個日常生活中的例子，從一個簡單的行為來理解這三者間的差異——**喝茶**。你為什麼喝茶？因為口渴。口渴是行為的原因。你希望透過喝茶達到什麼目的呢？想解渴。解渴是行為的目的。如果一切如期進行，你就可以達到你的目的，這杯茶確實可幫你解渴。但倘若喝了以後沒有解渴，反而讓你不舒服了呢？這就是行為的結果。大多時候事情會如期進行，行為的結果和目的會相符。然而，行為的結果和目的雖然會相符或有所重疊，並不表示兩者可混為一談。為了讓你理解此一論點，請看下列圖解：

好了，為了幫助你在商業情境下理解此一論點，讓我們來作另一道 Task 吧。不過這次請把焦點放在描述目的和結果的字串上。

TASK 4.2

請回到前一章的提案章節，閱讀 Task 3.11。將描述目的或描述結果的用語區分出來，並分別用不同顏色的筆將這兩類用語畫底線。

　　如果還不是很能理解目的和結果的區別，別擔心。請繼續往下研讀，你將會越來越明白。請先直接做下面的 Task，仔細研究 MWIs。

TASK 4.3

請將下列用語分類，填入下面的表格中。請利用 Task 3.11 的提案，幫助作答。

1. … in such a way as to V …
2. … in such a way that + n. clause …
3. … in order that + n. clause …
4. … in order to V …
5. From our experience, …
6. … lead to n.p. …
7. … otherwise + n. clause …
8. … result in n.p. …
9. … so as to V …
10. … so that + n. clause …
11. These strategies/recommendations will ensure that + n. clause …
12. This will result in n.p. …
13. This will V …
14. This strategy/recommendation will facilitate sth. in Ving
15. … to V …

Result	Purpose

答案 ▶

請利用下面的語庫核對答案。

提案 必備語庫 4.1 ▶

Result（結果）	Purpose（目的）
• This will result in n.p. … • This will V … • From our experience, … • These strategies/recommendations will ensure that + n. clause … • This strategy/recommendation will facilitate sth. in Ving • … lead to n.p. … • … result in n.p. … • … in such a way as to V … • … in such a way that + n. clause … • … otherwise + n. clause …	• … in order that + n. clause … • … in order to V … • … so as to V … • … so that + n. clause … • … to V …

★ 🗁 語庫小叮嚀

◆ Otherwise 永遠是用來指希望避免的結果。

◆ From our experience, … 很好用，可引介後面子句中所寫的結果。

好，現在我們來看此類字串在情境下的使用方式。其中表示目的的字串以粗體表示，表示結果的字串則以斜體表示。

Having spent a week in your office observing your staff going about the course of their daily duties, we would like to make the following preliminary proposals.

It is recommended that the cubicle height be lowered by five inches. Your staff should be able to see over the top of their partitions when seated. *This will facilitate management in checking that* their teams are

working efficiently.

We also suggest that your staff be allowed to personalize their cubicles with family photos and such personal objects. Obviously, the cubicles should not be so cluttered as to interfere with the work, but, *from our experience*, a degree of personalized office space improves moral and productivity.

Regarding the quality of the light, our recommendation here is that you change the neon strip lighting currently in use to a warmer and softer style of lighting. There also ought to be shades in front of the windows **so that** those workers currently sitting in direct afternoon sunlight can see their monitors. It is also proposed that some greenery be included in your office environment: having plants in the office often improves the air quality, and hence productivity.

We propose to conduct a follow-up visit **to assess** the effectiveness of our suggestions sometime in the next three months. However, we strongly recommend that these changes be carried out as soon as possible **so that** your business can start to function more effectively.

好,現在來了解一下許多人在使用此類字串時的通病,大部分的錯誤就如同我在前言中提到的一般:短字上出錯、字尾上出錯、set-phrases 的結尾上出錯,或者遺漏了 set-phrases 裡的幾個字。

為避免這些錯誤,請作下列 Task,確認你對語庫 4.1 的字串都熟悉了。

TASK 4.4
請利用語庫 4.1 重新改正以下句子的錯誤,寫出正確完整的句子,請看範例。

1. This will helping to reduce costs.
This will help to reduce costs.

2. This will result in that we can reduce costs.

3. From my experience to reduce costs.

4. These recommendation will ensure reducing costs.

5. This strategies will facilitate managers to reduce costs.

6. This will lead to we can reduce costs.

7. This will result in we can reduce costs.

8. We should adopt the proposal soon so reduce costs.

9. We should adopt the proposal soon to cost reduction.

10. We should implement the proposal soon in such a way as to reducing costs.

11. We should implement the proposal soon in such a way that reducing costs.

12. We should implement the proposal soon. Otherwise, we will reduce costs.

13. The proposal should be implemented soon in order that costs reduced.

14. The proposal should be implemented soon in order to reducing costs.

15. The proposal should be implemented soon so as to reducing costs.

答案 ▶

請看下面的正確答案。核對答案時，思考一下每個錯誤屬於哪一類，以避免日後重蹈覆轍。

2. This will result in reduced costs.

3. From my experience, this will reduce costs .

4. These recommendations will ensure that costs are reduced.

5. This strategy will facilitate management in reducing costs.

6. This will lead to a reduction in costs.

7. This will result in a reduction in costs.

8. We should adopt the proposal soon so as to reduce costs.

9. We should adopt the proposal soon to reduce costs.

10. We should implement the proposal soon in such a way as to reduce costs.

11. We should implement the proposal soon in such a way that costs are reduced.

12. We should implement the proposal soon. Otherwise, we will not be able to reduce costs.

13. The proposal should be implemented soon in order that costs can be reduced.

14. The proposal should be implemented soon in order to reduce costs.

15. The proposal should be implemented soon so as to reduce costs.

　　許多錯誤都在於，該使用 n. clause 的地方卻使用了 n.p.，或者該使用 n. clause 的地方卻使用了 V 。因此，在使用這些字串時，務必確定字串後所接的語法是正確的。

　　其他的錯誤則出現在 set-phrases 中，主詞的單複數型上，例如 this strategies 和 these recommendation，務必確認你都用對了。

描述假設情況及其結果

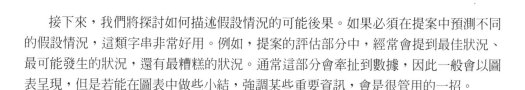

　　接下來，我們將探討如何描述假設情況的可能後果。如果必須在提案中預測不同的假設情況，這類字串非常好用。例如，提案的評估部分中，經常會提到最佳狀況、最可能發生的狀況，還有最糟糕的狀況。通常這部分會牽扯到數據，因此一般會以圖表呈現，但是若能在圖表中做些小結，強調某些重要資訊，會是很管用的一招。

TASK 4.5

請閱讀以下提案，並在你認為是描假設情況述和結果的字串下畫底線。

【背景說明】

　　惠特丹有限公司在台灣市場上生產草本牙膏。他們的牙膏在市場中是第二品牌，但期望在年底前拿下第一品牌的位子。焦點團體的初步研究顯示，大部分的消費者希望產品的香味能多一些。公司已出資進行一個規模較大的市場研究調查，但是行銷部主管已經按耐不住了，以下是她的建議提案。

> 　　My suggestion here is that we start to implement the proposal as soon as we can. If we delay the start until we receive the results of the market research, it's likely that our competitors will consolidate their lead and it will be even more difficult for us to steal market share. On the other hand, if we go ahead with the project and then the results of the market research are different from what we are expecting, we will not have lost much, as the early part of the project implementation doesn't involve much cost. However, it is more likely that the research will show what we have already learned from the preliminary focus groups. If it does, then we will already have saved some time by starting implementation early.

Word List

consolidate [kən`sɑlə,det] v. 鞏固；加強　　focus group　焦點團體
implementation [,ɪmpləmɛn`teʃən] n. 履行；完成

103

【提案摘要】

　　行銷部主管建議在收到市調前應盡快執行提案，以便搶先在競爭對手前取得多一點市場佔有率。就算執行後的市場狀況跟原本期望的市調結果有差距，也不會損失太多，因為初期的執行還不會動用到太多資金。而原本從焦點團體的初步研究學得的資訊，更可顯現在後來的市調上，若真是如此，則儘早執行確實可節省一些時間。

答案 ▶

稍後我們馬上回來細談這個練習，現在請先直接研讀語庫 4.2 中的字串和下面的例句。

提案 必備語庫 4.2 ▶

Conditions（假設語氣）	Consequences （結果）
• If we do that, … • If we V, … • If we don't V …, • Unless we V …, • Should we V …,	• … will V … • … may V … • … might V … • … could V … • … will probably V … • it will have the effect of Ving … • … may end up Ving … • it's likely that + n. clause … • … be likely to V … • there's every chance that + n. clause … • there's a strong possibility of n.p/Ving … • there is every/no/little likelihood of n.p./Ving … • there's every chance of n.p. … • it's possible that + n. clause … • it's unlikely that + n. clause … • there's a strong possibility that + n. clause … • … be unlikely to V … • there is every/no/little likelihood that + n. clause …

例句 ▶

1. If we adopt this proposal, it is likely that costs will fall.

2. Should we adopt this proposal, there's every chance that costs will fall.

3. Unless we make a big effort to attract new customers, it's unlikely that we can reach previous revenue levels.

4. It's likely that transport costs will increase if the price of oil doesn't come down.

★ 📁 語庫小叮嚀

◆ 請注意，每個例句均由表格中的兩欄組合而成；第一部分是描述假設情況，第二部分則是描述假設情況下的結果。

◆ 請注意，每個句子的第二部分都含有很多確定與不確定的未來式字串。這些字串，你在第二章中都已學過。

◆ 如果將假設語氣部分放在句首，句子的兩個部分間一定得用逗號隔開。如果把假設語氣部分放在句尾，則通常不可使用逗號。遵守這類小規則，可讓讀提案的 native speakers 留下深刻的印象。

◆ 假設語氣裡的 should 和 if 同義，在英式英文中較常見。

◆ 這裡的 Unless we V ..., 跟 If we don't V ..., 同義。

TASK 4.6

請回到 Task 4.5 的提案，在所有剛剛研讀過的字串下畫底線。請注意這些字串的用法。

答案 ▶

請利用語庫 4.2 來核對答案，但現在希望你已特別留意到逗號的用法，以及每一個句子中有兩種子句的寫法。接下來我們就來學習如何使用這類字串吧。

TASK 4.7

請利用下面的 word partnerships 和語庫 4.2 中的字串，寫出關於假設情況和結果的句子。在開始之前，請先看範例。

1.	employ untrained staff	reduce our wage bill
2.	keep larger stocks	run out of merchandise
3.	update the computer system	save money
4.	take on more staff	reduce the workload
5.	reduce prices	damage the brand
6.	freeze wages	damage morale
7.	cut costs	reduce quality
8.	invest in new equipment	reduce production time
9.	restructure the department	lay off some staff
10.	merge with a competitor	increase our market share

例句 ▶

1. If we employ more untrained staff, it will have the effect of reducing our wage bill.

答案 ▶

這些句子的寫法顯然有很多種，端視你選擇使用的 MWIs 而定，但是請看一看我在下面提供的建議答案。閱讀時，建議你一邊看，一邊在字串底下畫線，以幫助你將焦點放在這些 MWIs 的用法上。

2. If we don't keep larger stocks, we may end up running out of merchandise.
3. Unless we update the computer system, we may not be able to save money in the long term.
4. Should we take on more staff, we will reduce the current workload.
5. If we reduce prices, there's every chance that this will damage the brand.
6. If we freeze wages, it will have the effect of damaging morale in the company.

merchandise ['mɜtʃən͵daɪz] *n.* 貨物；商品
take on 雇用（員工）

workload ['wɜk͵lod] *n.* 工作量
lay off 解雇

7. Should we cut costs, it's possible that quality will be reduced.
8. If we invest in new equipment now, there's every chance that in the long run we can reduce production time.
9. If we restructure the department, there's every likelihood that we will need to lay off some staff.
10. If we merge with our main competitor, there's a strong possibility of increasing our market share.

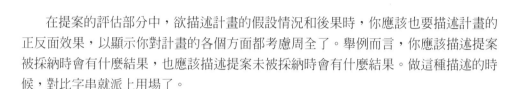

以對比字串做正反面的評估

　　在提案的評估部分中，欲描述計畫的假設情況和後果時，你應該也要描述計畫的正反面效果，以顯示你對計畫的各個方面都考慮周全了。舉例而言，你應該描述提案被採納時會有什麼結果，也應該描述提案未被採納時會有什麼結果。做這種描述的時候，對比字串就派上用場了。

TASK 4.8

請再看一次 Task 4.5 裡的提案，並在你認為的對比字串下畫底線。

答案 ▶

請以下列語庫 4.3 核對答案。

提案 必備語庫 4.3 ▶

• However, ...	• On the contrary, ...
• On the other hand, ...	• By contrast, ...
• Still, ...	• Then again, ...

TASK 4.9

現在回到前面的 Task 4.7，在你已經寫下的句子中加入對比句。請看範例。

例句 ▶

　　If we employ more untrained staff, it will have the effect of reducing our wage bill. **On the other hand**, our training costs are likely to rise if we want to maintain the quality of the products.

答案 ▶

　　同樣地，我不知道你在這個練習中寫了什麼答案，不過以下提供我的答案供你參考。請閱讀這些答案，並注意對比字串的用法。

2. If we don't keep larger stocks, we may end up running out of merchandise. **However**, keeping larger stocks means increased inventory costs.

3. Unless we update the computer system, we may not be able to save money in the long term. **On the other hand**, if we spend this money now we will have a better computer system and save money in the long term.

4. Should we take on more staff, we will reduce the current workload. **Then again**, this will result in increased wage costs.

5. If we reduce prices, there's every chance that this will damage the brand. **On the contrary**, if we don't reduce prices, it will be difficult to increase sales volume.

6. If we freeze wages, it will have the effect of damaging morale in the company. **By contrast**, if we freeze wages for six months, we will save some money in the short term.

7. Should we cut costs, it's possible that quality will be reduced. **Still**, cutting costs in areas other than production should be attempted.

8. If we invest in new equipment now, there's every chance that in the long run we can reduce production time. **However**, this will of course involve some initial capital expenditure.

9. If we restructure the department, there's every likelihood that we will need to lay off some staff. **Then again**, if we don't restructure the department, we will continue to lose money through inefficiencies.

10. If we merge with our main competitor, there's a strong possibility of increasing our market share. **On the other hand**, merging will alter the character of the company and bring a different set of problems.

TASK 4.10

請閱讀下列提案中的評估部分，用兩種不同顏色的筆分別將描述假設情況和結果的字串，以及對比字串畫底線。

W o r d   L i s t

attempted [ə`tɛmptɪd] *adj.* 企圖達到的

capital [`kæpətl] *n.* 資金

alter [`ɔltə] *v.* 改變；變更

character [`kærɪktə] *n.* (東西的)特質；特性

【背景說明】

　　Stealbucks 是一間在台灣北部各地均設有零售店的頂級咖啡公司。他們的主要競爭對手最近推出一項產品，幾乎和他們自己的招牌咖啡一模一樣，而且因為比較便宜，競爭對手已成功搶走了 Stealbucks 的一些顧客，Stealbucks 的銷售量因此而一瀉千里。以下是該公司行銷經理對處理問題的建議。

> 　　My recommendation here is that we reduce the price of our main product by 2%. If we don't, there's a strong possibility that our competitors will steal some of our main customers for this product. It has been pointed out to me that should we reduce the price, we could damage the brand. On the contrary, my view is that the brand is already in danger and that we need to hold on to our main customers by reducing the price and maintaining brand loyalty.

【提案摘要】

　　該名經理建議將主力產品的價格調降 2%，雖然有人指出調降售價將對品牌有害，但他卻不這麼認為，就因為品牌已經岌岌可危了，所以更應該降價來留住主要的客戶，以及維持品牌忠誠度。

答案

請用下列文章核對答案。假設情況和結果的字串以粗體表示，對比字串以斜體表示。

> 　　My recommendation here is that we reduce the price of our main product by 2%. **If we don't, there's a strong possibility that** our competitors will steal some of our main customers for this product. It has been pointed out to me that **should we** reduce the price, **we could** damage the brand. *On the contrary*, my view is that the brand is already in danger and that we need to hold on to our main customers by reducing the price and maintaining brand loyalty.

view [vju] *n.* 看法；觀點

延伸寫作

請從第三章的延伸寫作中選出一個已描述過的問題，評估自己的建議。請試著利用你在本章中學過的字串。

參考答案 1

Office Environment Memo

At the moment I think the office environment is hurting our productivity. It is too dark, the air quality is not good, and some employees are frustrated by their inability to stay in touch with business contacts overseas. I have three main recommendations to make in order to improve the situation. First, I recommend that we replace the windows with clear glass so that we can see out of the window and get more light. If we do that, some people may end up looking out of the window a lot instead of working. However, more daylight will make it easier to see what we are doing. Secondly, we should have air conditioning so as to keep the office at a comfortable temperature all year round. If we don't put in air conditioning soon, there's every chance that employee absenteeism will increase during the hot summer months as it will be too hot to work. Thirdly, we ought to have individual access to the Internet. Because we are doing more business over the Internet these days, I think every computer in the office should be connected, rather than just two. I understand your concern about people using office equipment to browse the Internet. Still, this recommendation will ensure that we are not losing business because foreign customers cannot contact us easily.

【提案摘要】

針對辦公室太暗，空氣品質不好，以及無法與國外客戶保持聯繫的問題，有三點

W o r d　L i s t

inability [ˌɪnəˈbɪlətɪ] *n.* 無能力

absenteeism [ˌæbsn̩ˈtiɪzm̩] *n.* 曠課；曠工

browse [braʊs] *v.* 瀏覽（網站）

建議。第一，建議將窗戶的玻璃換成透明玻璃，這樣一來，員工可看看窗外，光線也會較為充足。雖然這樣會讓員工看窗外的時間多過於真正工作的時間，但多點陽光仍是好的。第二，指出若不趕快加裝空調，可能會讓員工的夏季缺席率提高。第三，指出雖然有人會利用公司的設備來上網，但每個人的電腦還是都得有網路連結，以免因聯繫不易而流失掉外國客戶。

參考答案 2

Line Management: A Proposal

I feel that the management of my position is not clear, so I would like to make the following recommendations. Currently for overseas business, I report to our regional office, and for domestic business I report to our Taipei Sales Director, while for everyday business activities, I report to the Kaohsiung Office Manager. My proposal here is that I report directly to the Taipei Sales Director only, as most of my work is domestic. If I have international business to conduct, I suggest that I report this to the Taipei Sales Director as well, who can then pass my report up to regional office. These recommendations will ensure that I spend more time on my job, rather than spending time thinking about who I should report to. Also, should we make the lines of management clearer, I think that it's unlikely that the big problems we had last month will be repeated.

【提案摘要】

由於覺得此職位的管理不清楚，這是因為針對不同的業務需向不同的主管提出報告，因此提議直接提報給台北的業務主管即可，若有國外業務，可請台北業務主管傳遞給區辦公室。這樣可將更多時間投注在工作上，而不是花時間在想該跟誰報告。此外，若能將管理的流程弄得更清楚些，此後上個月的問題就不大可能會再發生了。

好，提案中評估部分的學習到此結束。在完成本章之前，請回到本章引言中的學習清單，確認每個項目都確實理解了。

Part **2**
撰寫英文報告

Report

Unit 5

如何寫出效果佳的
英文報告

引言與學習目標

我們在本書的第一部分中，詳細探討了提案的寫法；在本書的第二部分中，我們則要來學習撰寫各種不同的報告。報告基本上可分為兩類：一類是以時間為主軸的定期報告，例如年、季或月報告；另一類是為特定事件寫的特定報告，例如聯繫報告和專案進度報告。

一般定期報告中使用的用語和你在第二章學到的用語可以說是如出一轍，也就是將報告分成現在、過去、未來三個部分來寫，每個部分的時間 chunks 和動詞時態務必搭配正確。如果你仔細研讀了第二章，寫定期報告便應該是小事一樁了。不過特定報告要求的用語不同，這我會在第六章（專案進度報告）和第七章（聯繫報告）中談到。

許多報告會以表格和圖表等格式提供財務數據，有時你也可能有必要以文字敘述表格和圖表中的某些數字。此外，特別強調一些特定的財務資訊，這個做法也很有效。這時很重要的一點，就是能夠祭出精準反應表格和圖表內容的用語，這些用語你也會在第八章（財務報告）中學到。

本章結束時，各位應達成的學習目標如下：

- ❑ 對報告的目的有更清楚的了解。
- ❑ 更瞭解報告目的如何決定內容和用語。
- ❑ 知道報告的寫作過程為何。
- ❑ 學到一些實用的報告呈現技巧，例如分段和條列式寫法。
- ❑ 學到一些實用的寫作技巧，如標點符號、日期、時間、稱謂和姓名的寫法。

報告的寫作目的

TASK 5.1

請思考以下問題,如有必要請做筆記。

寫商業報告的目的為何?

答案

我相信你的答案多半會是:提供讀者商業活動的相關資訊。這個答案當然沒有錯,然而你的商業報告如要真正令人印象深刻,我們同時也得思考報告寫作的幾個其他目的,而這些目的也同等重要。

1. 除了提供讀者商業活動的相關資訊,報告應該被視為是進一步推銷公司、服務和產品的機會。如果報告的讀者是顧客或策略夥伴,這一點更不容忽視。

2. 報告應該被視為是另一個推銷自己,以及展現自己商業能力和語文能力的大好機會。

3. 報告中也應該提供事件紀錄。如果你的團隊正在進行的專案有多個不同的商業團體參與,例如大家一起合夥投資、形成策略聯盟或一起為客戶提供服務,那麼你應該在報告中提供一份紀錄,以便在執行專案的下一步驟前獲得各方共識。

4. 如此看來,報告也可視為是一種法律文件。若你和合夥人、顧客或供應商的關係亮起了紅燈,這份報告即是法律糾紛中有力的證據。

由此可見,報告中的資訊和用語務必精確而真實。

報告的寫作過程

　　現在我們來看一下報告的寫作過程。在第一章中我提過蒐集資訊、衡量資訊和呈現資訊的過程，許多我在當時所教的內容印證在報告的寫作上都很受用，但只有一處不同。寫提案時之所以必須衡量呈現出來的資訊是否和計畫有關，是因為你的提案是針對現在或未來的需求，亦即提案是具有前瞻性的。然而在報告中，你必須呈現的是所有已發生的事情，因為報告是回顧性的；報告談的是過去已發生的事情。因此，報告的寫作過程主要有下列三點：

1. 首先列出所有必須放進報告的資訊。列出資訊時應該要保持誠實的態度，不管正面或負面的資訊都得老實地列出來。舉幾個例子，如果你的銷售成績不理想、沒有達成目標、或者進度有些落後，這些都必須在報告中一五一十地交代清楚。不要企圖隱瞞事實，你要做的應該是在報告中解釋這些負面事件的發生原因、你打算如何彌補劣勢、還有將採取哪些行動避免重蹈覆轍。

2. 一旦決定要在報告中放進哪些資訊和做好資訊清單後，接下來便應該將資訊分段整理，而這些段落即為你報告最終版本的分段依據。在重新整理資訊時易犯的最大錯誤，就是用找到資訊或想法形成的時間先後來排序，殊不知找到資訊或想法形成的先後順序，對讀者來說其實不見得是最妥當的閱讀順序。你可以選擇根據時間，如季、月或年來安排段落，或者按照地區或商業活動來整理報告。無論你安排資訊的順序為何，請確定讀者在閱讀時順序是清楚並符合邏輯的。

3. 整理好想法和決定好報告架構後，就可以動筆寫作了。此時需要注意的是語言的精準度，此時你要做的便是將本書教過的用語，和接下來幾章中即將學到的所有知識實際運用在寫作上。

　　以下提供許多我的學生認為有用的技巧，供你寫報告時參考。

- 關掉電腦中的文法檢查功能。這個功能準確率低，容易讓人困惑，也高度的不可

靠,只要善用你自本書學到的知識,即可判斷所使用的文法是否正確。至於拼字檢查功能則可保留下來,以便檢查打字有無出錯。

- 請悉心校對你的報告。寫完報告後再仔細地閱讀一遍,抓出拼字、打字等錯誤。我每次都會把最後的檢查留到第二天再做,不知道為什麼,感覺上隔一些時間後我挑出的錯誤會比較多。

- 我服務過的公司大部分都有報告的寫作範本。這些範本經常以表格的方式編排,你可以按照範本輕而易舉地寫出報告。如果你的公司也是這種作法,那麼你便得以按照範本整理資料,然後專心校對報告中的各個部分或表格中的用語。

- 許多人擔心報告寫得不夠正式,他們會有這樣的疑慮是因為報告不只是一種記錄,也是一種法律文件,感覺上應該寫得一板一眼、禮數周到。這個觀念大錯特錯,其實只要使用日常的商業用語即可。報告是提供資訊的文件,用到的資訊性用語多、溝通性用語少。請不要擔心報告的用語是否正式或禮數周到,準確度才是重點,亦即資訊和語言的準確度。

- 報告的長度沒有特定規定,該寫多長就寫多長,該寫多短就多短。一般考慮報告長度時,端視希望放進多少資訊而定。盡量保持句子的簡潔。與其寫一個複雜的長句,倒不如將其拆解成兩個簡短的句子,比較好閱讀也比較容易寫。報告中的用語應清楚明瞭,讓讀者可以專心思考語言所欲傳達的資訊,而不因用語複雜而分心。如果為了做到這一點,你每份報告都使用類似的字串也沒關係,只要每次都使用正確即可。寫報告的目標是傳達商業資訊,而不是寫出華麗的英文詞藻!

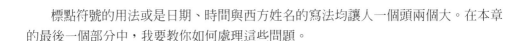

標點符號、日期、時間等寫法

　　標點符號的用法或是日期、時間與西方姓名的寫法均讓人一個頭兩個大。在本章的最後一個部分中，我要教你如何處理這些問題。

1. 標點符號。英文寫作中所使用的標點符號均是半形的英文字體，而非全形的中文字體。在這裡特別要注意的是分號的用法，如果不確定什麼時候該用分號，就不要胡亂使用。（其實商業寫作很少用到分號，所以乾脆一個都別用！）此外，行與行間不需再多空一行，這種格式已經老掉牙了。這種小細節累積多了，會讓你的讀者留下不好的印象。

2. 日期。這裡我提供幾個慣用寫法，供你參考。美國人通常會把月寫在前面，然後是日，最後才是年，年月日中間則以斜線（5/17/05）或連字號（5-17-05）隔開。英國、紐、澳和歐洲一些其他國家則習慣先寫日，再寫月，最後才寫年，年月日中間則是以句點分隔開來（17.05.2005）。此外，你也可以將月份用英文表示，如 May 17, 2005 或 17 May 2005。請注意，美式寫法是以逗號分隔日期和年，英式寫法則一個逗號都不用。

3. 時間。你可以用二十四小時制來寫，如 13：30；或者以十二小時制來寫，但須加上 a.m. 或 p.m.，如 01：30 p.m.（p.m. 表示中午以後，a.m. 表示午夜以後，中午 12 點則用 12：00 p.m.）。由於日期和時間的寫法多不勝數，我的建議是：瞭解你們公司其他人的寫法為何，照他們的方式來寫即可。此外，應注意的是，同一份報告中的寫法應前後一致。

4. 姓名。許多以中文為母語的人覺得西方人姓名的寫法複雜難懂。別擔心，因為對西方人而言，中文姓名的寫法更令他們頭大！大部分的西方人有三個名字，第一個通常是名（ex. Quentin），最後一個通常是姓（ex. Brand），中間的那個名字平常則幾乎用不到（我的是 Thomas）。因此我的全名就是 Quentin Thomas Brand ，中間不需任何逗點。看看本書封面上我的名字擺法，即可一目了然。

5. 稱謂。稱謂永遠是和姓一起使用，如：Mr. Brand，而不是 Mr. Quentin。稱呼別人時，男性用 Mr.，已婚女性用 Mrs.，未婚女性則使用 Ms.。在西方國家裡，許多女性不認為婚姻身分和稱謂有任何關係，因此無論是否已婚，均用 Ms.，我也建議使用 Ms. 會比較恰當。在美式寫法中，Mr.、Mrs. 和 Ms. 後面永遠會接一個句點，代表是縮寫的意思。但在英式寫法中則不加句點。不論你在稱謂的後面是否使用句點，同一文件中的寫法前後一致即可。其他的稱謂還包括 Dr.（醫生或博士）、Pr.（教授，這個稱謂在歐洲國家比較常見）。西方國家的人通常不會以他人在公司的頭銜來稱呼對方，例如，我們不會說 Vice President Brand（Brand 副總裁），就算我是副總裁或執行長（CEO），你還是應該叫我 Mr. Brand。用姓來稱呼對方卻不使用稱謂，聽起來有欠禮數，如：Brand is coming on Friday.「Brand 禮拜五要來。」，因此不建議使用。

最後，為完整學習本章，本段要教你的技巧就是將資訊分段，請注意，報告最重要的任務就是易於閱讀。因此，你可使用條列式、編號或破折號將資訊分段。現在我們來做一個 Task，你就會瞭解我的意思了。

TASK 5.2

請閱讀下列兩段文字，試著從這兩個版本中找出提到公司文件範本的地方，哪一個版本比較容易閱讀？哪一個版本比較容易找到所需的資訊？

範例 1 ▶

- Turn off the Microsoft grammar checker on your computer. It is inaccurate, confusing and very, very unreliable. Instead, rely on the knowledge you have gained from this book. Leave the spell checker on, however, and use it only to tidy up your typing.

- Make sure you edit your work carefully. Read it through carefully after you

---

W o r d   L i s t

checker [ˋtʃɛkə] n. 檢查員；審查者
inaccurate [ɪnˋækjərɪt] adj. 不精確的

unreliable [͵ʌnrɪˋlaɪəb!] adj. 不可靠的
tidy up 收拾；使整潔

have written it so that you can see the spelling, typing and other errors. I always leave this final check till the next day: for some reason I seem to find more mistakes if some time has passed!

• Most companies that I have worked with have templates for report writing. These often take the form of tables which you have to complete, or document templates which you simply follow. If this is the case for your company, then you need to organize your information into the template, and then focus on the language you are using for each section of the template or table.

範例 2 ▶

Turn off the Microsoft grammar checker on your computer. It is inaccurate, confusing and very, very unreliable. Instead, rely on the knowledge you have gained from this book. Leave the spell checker on, however, and use it only to tidy up your typing. Make sure you edit your work carefully. Read it through carefully after you have written it so that you can see the spelling, typing and other errors. I always leave this final check till the next day: for some reason I seem to find more mistakes if some time has passed! Most companies that I have worked with have templates for report writing. These often take the form of tables which you have to complete, or document templates which you simply follow. If this is the case for your company, then you need to organize your information into the template, and then focus on the language you are using for each section of the template or table.

答案 ▶

希望你看得出來：第一個版本較易閱讀並尋找所需資訊，因為它使用了條列式寫法而且段落分明。請記住，報告的呈現方式也應該像這樣方便讀者找資訊，報告架構也需顯而易見。

template [ˋtɛmplɪt] *n.* 供人依循的格式範本   table [ˋtebl] *n.* 表格

　　好，本章的學習到此結束，閱讀量很大，但希望本章教的技巧和提供的知識對你是有幫助的。在接下來的三章中，我們會做比較多的語言練習，因此在繼續往下學習之前，請回到本章前面的學習清單，確定所有項目都已確實吸收了。

Unit 6 ─────────

專案進度報告

引言與學習目標

在本章中，我們要學習的是撰寫描述特定狀況的報告。專案進度報告是一種商業職場上常見且重要的報告。新專案的推出有著推動公司發展的目的，透過這類報告，母公司或高階經理可以控管新專案的進度。報告上面的資訊應包括目前的進度是到哪一階段、哪些階段落後了、過程中遇到了哪些問題、以及市場狀況的變化為何。因此，這類報告中的資訊和用語務求精準和直接，如果你是專案主導人，身負撰寫專案進度報告的重任，此時也正是你展現管理和語言技能的最佳機會。

專案進度報告的架構應該依照計畫的特質而定。例如：你可以依據段落來解說參與計畫的各部門正在進行的事項，也可以根據時間點安排報告內容。不管你決定使用哪一種架構，大部分的專案進度報告均具備三大元素：一、**描述已完成的事項**，說明哪些任務已經達成。二、**描述未完成的事項**，說明寫報告當下正在進行的任務。三、**描述未來的計畫和安排**，說明專案下一階段的任務。

本章的教學重點即是將這三大元素的用語傳授給你。許多用語和你在第二章學到的動詞時態有異曲同工之妙，所以在繼續往下學習本章前，建議你回頭快速複習一下在第二章中做過的 Task。

本章結束時，各位應達成的學習目標如下：

- ❑ 對專案進度報告中應該放進哪些資訊已有些概念。
- ❑ 對安排報告資訊的方法有更多的了解。
- ❑ 有能力描述專案中已經完成的事項。
- ❑ 有能力描述專案中正在進行的事項。
- ❑ 有能力描述專案下一階段的任務。

報告中應囊括的三大部分

我們先由研讀專案進度報告開始。

TASK 6.1

請閱讀下列報告,想一想下列問題並作筆記。

1. 報告的安排方式為何?
2. 你注意到主要的時態是哪些了嗎?

【背景說明】

　　ASPAC 銀行是一家區域性銀行和信用卡發行機構,總公司位於新加坡。台灣是該行第二大的信用卡區域市場,他們在台灣信用卡市場中排名第四。他們即將推出的新信用卡目標鎖定在 18 到 25 歲的族群,公司希望在推出信用卡後的六個月內攻下市場第二名的位子。以下是寫給總公司的專案進度報告。

"Easy Debt" New Credit Card Launch
Project Status Report December 12, 2005

Overview

　　In the last three months since the project was given the go-ahead, the market situation has changed somewhat. Two of our main competitors have launched similar products, much to our surprise. However, market indications are that their products are not performing as well on the market as they hoped. At the last project status review meeting (November 4) it was agreed by all parties to continue the "Easy Debt" project notwithstanding the increased competitiveness of

---

W o r d　L i s t

go-ahead [ˋgo əˏhɛd] *n.* 許可;核准
indication [ˏɪndəˋkeʃən] *n.* 跡象;暗示

party [ˋpɑrtɪ] *n.* 關係人;當事人
notwithstanding [ˏnɑtwɪθˋstændɪŋ] *prep.* 儘管

the market. We are watching the overall marketing of their products very carefully to see what lessons we can learn from any mistakes. The launch date for "Easy Debt" is still expected to be April 1st.

Marketing

Working with our media company, we've finalized the strategy for the launch.

- We've already booked key billboards around town for the launch period, and we've also just bought airtime on five radio stations and two major TV channels. We are within budget so far on media buying, as we've managed to negotiate a 20% discount on radio airtime (see accompanying data). Our plan is to allocate those funds to the press launch party, which we intend to make one of the social/press events of the year.
- We've made all the arrangements for the press launch at the Big Fancy Hotel On The Hill. Our intention is to invite a couple of famous pop-stars to join us. We're meeting with the F&B manager tomorrow to finalize the menu.
- We're taking steps to ensure good media coverage of the launch, and hope to have more details for the next report.

Advertising is on track.

- We've received the copy for the print ads from our agency, and it has been tested with focus groups with good results, so that's done.
- We've decided to use a slightly younger model for the print ads and TV commercial, but we haven't yet found a face suitable for the concept, so that still needs to be done. We've been looking at portfolios from various different modeling agencies, but we are still trying to

airtime [ˈɛr͵taɪm] *n.* 播出時間
allocate [ˈælə͵ket] *v.* 分派；分配

F&B (Food & Beverage) manager 餐飲經理
coverage [ˈkʌvərɪdʒ] *n.* （廣播、電視的）播放範圍

agree on the final choice. We're going to finalize this by the end of the week.

- We're having problems with the script for the TV commercial. Our marketing department and the agency are still not in agreement about the audio, so that still needs more work.

- The design of the card has now been completed, and the manufacturer is ready to start production, so that's ready to go.

Back office

We are still looking for a manager.

- We haven't managed to recruit a manager for the back office end of the project, but HR is working round the clock on this. In the meantime, Operations VP Sung is acting manager.

Training and support planning is underway.

- Right now we are in the middle of training call center staff to deal with the new card.

- Also we're in the process of completing the last touches to the new computer systems which are going to handle all the data. However, because of the shortage of programmers we have been a bit delayed, so that's not ready yet.

- We've made arrangements to train 20 field officers from partner institutions who will then be responsible for training their own staff. We have managed to save some of our training budget by doing this, and we are making arrangements to reallocate this budget to the TV commercial.

W o r d   L i s t

round the clock 不間斷地；日以繼夜地   call center 客戶服務中心

VP (vice president) 副總裁

【報告摘要】

概要

　　暨此專案在幾個月前推出後，競爭對手也推出了相似的產品，雖然他們的商品表現不如他們預期的好，對我們而言競爭也增加了，但在上次的會議中，大家仍同意此專案應繼續推行。

行銷部門

與媒體公司溝通過後，推行策略已經定案

- 為宣傳期定了廣告看板：買了五個電台的廣播時段以及兩個電視頻道，目前預算還在控制之內，因此希望將廣播經費再降 20%，預計將這些資金分配到媒體造勢派對上，做一個年度的社交造勢活動。
- 已為派對預定好飯店，將邀請一些當紅巨星參加，明天將訂定菜單。
- 確保宣傳期有良好的媒體覆蓋率。

廣告已在推行

- 焦點團體已測試完傳單的效果，結果良好。
- 平面傳單跟電視廣告已決定要用年輕一點的模特兒，但還沒找到合適人選，目前已著手在不同模特兒經紀公司中尋找，預計本週末定案。
- 對電視廣告的腳本有不同的意見，目前還在協商中。
- 卡的樣式已完成，也已準備生產。

後勤辦公室

聘任新的經理

- 人資部已著手招募新的經理

訓練和支援企劃都已在進行

- 目前正訓練新卡的客服人員
- 處理資料的軟體已幾近完成，但由於工程師短缺，因此這部分會有點延遲。
- 已經安排訓練 20 個商業伙伴的員工，之後他們可自行訓練自己的員工，以降低人事預算。

答案 ▶

相信你已經看出來了，這份報告有三大部分。Overview 描述的是專案的進度概況，以及市場狀況的改變對專案的影響。接著，報告將重點放在專案的兩個主要參與部門上——行銷部門和後勤辦公室。報告中也提及其他參與者在此次專案中扮演的角色，

如：承接案子的廣告公司和媒體購買公司。需特別注意的是，報告用條列式寫法逐項列明內容，這個技巧我在第五章中已經教過。

　　就用語來說，由於報告提到的時期尚未結束（從 11 月 4 日至今），因此所使用的動詞多半是現在進行式或是現在完成式，看得出來嗎？報告中簡單過去式用的不多，若有也全部是指過去已完成的特定事件，例如上次開會的日期。

描述已完成／未完成事項的用語

現在我們就繼續深入研讀專案進度報告的用語。先來看一看我稍早提到的前兩個語言項目——描述已完成事項的用語，以及描述未完成事項的用語。

TASK 6.2

請將下列用語分門別類，填入下表中。

1. … so that still needs more work.
2. … so that still needs to be done.
3. … so that's done.
4. … so that's not ready yet.
5. … so that's ready to go.
6. … has now been completed.
7. … has now been finalized.
8. … we have been a bit delayed.
9. Right now we're in the middle of Ving …
10. We are working round the clock on this.
11. We haven't managed to V yet.

12. We haven't p.p. yet …
13. We're having problems with n.p. …
14. We're in the process of Ving …
15. We're trying to V …
16. We've already p.p. …
17. We've been able to V …
18. We've been Ving …
19. We've decided to V …
20. We've just p.p. …
21. We've managed to V …
22. We've p.p. …

Describing Completed Results	Describing Uncompleted Activities

答案 ▶

請利用下面的語庫核對答案。

提案 必備語庫 6.1 ▶

Describing Completed Results （描述已完成的結果）	Describing Uncompleted Activities （描述未完成的活動）
• We've p.p. … • We've just p.p. … • We've already p.p. … • We've managed to V … • We've decided to V … • We've been able to V … • … so that's done. • … so that's ready to go. • … has now been finalized. • … has now been completed.	• We've been Ving … • We're trying to V … • We're in the process of Ving … • We are working round the clock on this. • We haven't p.p. yet … • We haven't managed to V yet. • We're having problems with n.p. … • We're having problems Ving … • Right now we're in the middle of Ving … • … so that's not ready yet. • … so that still needs more work. • … so that still needs to be done. • … we have been a bit delayed.

★🗁 語庫小叮嚀

◆ 請注意句首用了哪些 set-phrases，句尾又用了哪些 set-phrases。

◆ 請注意動詞時態：肯定的現在完成式表示已完成的事項，而現在進行式
和否定的現在完成式則表示未完成的事項。

◆ 另外也請注意，報告中的有些句子會同時使用兩個 set-phrases，一個
放在句首，另一個放在句尾，如：We haven't yet found a face suitable
for the concept, so that still needs to be done.。

TASK 6.3

請再閱讀一次 Task 6.1 中的報告，找出語庫 6.1 中所有的用語，並劃底線。請注意這
些字串的用法。

希望做完這個 Task 後,你對報告用語的瞭解又更上一層樓了。既然你已能掌握不同字串的意思,想必你對分辨任務是否已經完成的感覺應更敏銳了。

好,現在我們就來練習運用這些字串。

TASK 6.4

請看活動經理為 Easy Debt Launch 專案所做的筆記。請利用語庫 6.1 中的用語分別幫已完成的事項和預計完成的事項造出完整句,讓活動經理可在下一份專案進度報告中使用。請看範例。

Things Already Done (已完成的事項)	Things to Finish (預計完成的事項)
1. decide on the menu	**a)** send out invitations
2. check the budget for dinner	**b)** complete guest list
3. print invitations	**c)** find and book some entertainment
4. prepare banners and posters for the dining room	**d)** ensure TV coverage

例句 ▶

1. We've already decided on the menu, so that's done.

答案 ▶

請看下列所提供的建議答案。當然,你用的字串可能不同,沒關係,只要記得仔細檢查每個字串的細節,以及字串間的連接詞跟句子的其他部分是正確的即可。

已完成的事項:

2. We've already decided on the menu.

3. We've managed to prepare banners and posters for the dining room.

Word List

banner [ˋbænə] *n.* 旗幟
poster [ˋpostə] *n.* 海報;廣告

ensure [ɪnˋʃʊr] *v.* 保證;使安全

4. We've got the invitations printed, so they're ready to go.

預計完成的事項：

a) We're in the middle of sending out the invitations.

b) We haven't managed to complete the guest list, so that still needs to be done.

c) We're in the process of finding and booking some entertainment.

d) We're still trying to ensure good TV coverage.

描述未來的計畫或安排

　　現在繼續往下學習，我之前提過的第三種語言項目——描述下一階段任務的用語。你可能還記得，在第二章中我教過你兩種未來式： personal 和 impersonal，我們也練習過用 impersonal 的未來式描述對商業概況的預測。在本節中，我們則要學習 personal 的未來用語。由於你正在進行的專案牽涉到你個人、你的團隊和你認識的人，因此報告中勢必得用 personal 的未來用語來描述各種未來的計畫和安排。

TASK 6.5

請研讀下列語庫，然後再重新閱讀一次 Task 6.1 中的報告，找出這些 MWIs 並注意 MWIs 的用法。

提案 必備語庫 6.2 ▶

Describing Arrangements (描述安排的事項)
• We're going to V ...
• We're Ving ...
• We're taking steps to V ...
• We intend to V ...
• We're making arrangements for n.p. ...
• We're making arrangements to V ...
• We've made arrangements for n.p. ...
• We've made arrangements to V ...
• Our intention is to V ...
• Our plan is to V ...
• We hope to V ...
• We've still got to V ...
• We plan to V ...

★ 🗀 語庫小叮嚀

　　◆ 需注意的是，我們不用 will 來描述未來的計畫或安排。別小看這個規則，以中文為母語的人士在使用英文時便常犯下這種錯誤。大部分的人

> 在說寫各種未來式時，常濫用 will 一詞。談個人未來的計畫和安排時，盡量少用 will。如果記得這個規則，減少 will 的使用次數，這個小小的改變將可讓讀者對你的英語能力留下極深刻的印象。
>
> ◆ 請特別留意語庫中有 arrangements 一詞的 set-phrases ，因為這種用語很難掌握。雖然某個事件是未來才會發生，但你應該根據該事件是否已安排好而決定該用現在進行式或現在完成式。

現在我們就來練習使用這些字串。

TASK 6.6

請看活動經理為下一份專案進度報告所做的筆記，並請寫下他可以在報告中用上的句子。請看範例。

Things to Do
1. ask ASPAC Taiwan general manager to make a speech
2. prepare gift packs for each guest
3. work out the budget for gift packs
4. press release
5. organize firework display

例句 ▶

1. Our plan is to ask the ASPAC Taiwan general manager to make a speech.

答案 ▶

請看下列所提供的建議答案。當然，你用的字串可能不同，不過沒關係。只要記得仔細檢查字串的細節，以及之間的連接詞跟句子的其他部分是正確的即可。此外，也請確認你在寫這些未來計畫的句子中，沒有用到任何的 will。

2. We are going to prepare gift packs for each guest.
3. We've still got to work out the budget for gift packs.
4. We're making arrangements for the press release.
5. We hope to organize a firework display.

Word List

release [rɪˋlis] *n.* 新聞等（發表）；新聞稿

137

好，現在來看一看你能否在有上下文的情境中正確地使用這些句子。

TASK 6.7

請在這份專案進度報告的空格中填入適當的字串。有些空格的正確答案不只一個。

【背景說明】

Infosys 是一家位於新竹科學園區的系統建造與設計公司。這家公司成立不久，野心勃勃。他們專門生產量身訂做的 CRM（客戶關係管理）軟體程式。目前的客戶是一家五星級的連鎖精品飯店，這家飯店在亞洲太平洋地區設有八家分店，這可說是 Infosys 的大好機會。以下即 Infosys 專案經理寫給執行長的報告。

Laguna Hotels Project Status Report
Confidential

Overview

The project is on schedule so far, but a little over budget. The relationship with the new client is developing nicely, and I feel that trust is growing from their IT manager, who was initially against the project.

Progress so far

- ____(1)____ (receive) the clear brief from the client about their needs, and ____(2)____ (discuss) as a team how to meet those requirements. ____(3)____ (submit) our proposal to them, ____(4)____ , and an action plan ____(5)____ .
- ____(6)____ employ two new programmers so that we can be sure to get this project finished on time, and ____(7)____ brief them on the project too.
- ____(8)____ get the client's database and ____(9)____ study it to see whether the data can be organized in a more efficient

---

W o r d   L i s t

confidential [ˌkɑnfəˈdɛnʃəl] *adj.* 祕密的；機密的   database [ˈdetəˌbes] *n.* 資料庫

way according to their needs.

Current status

- _____(10)_____ working out new pathways through their data and _____(11)_____ designing new links to different sets of information.
- We've had some problems with data storage capacity, so _____(12)_____ (build in) extra capacity as we go, but _____(13)_____ (finished) this yet.
- The new links are still not working smoothly, _____(14)_____ .
- _____(15)_____ designing the new user interface, as the client wasn't happy with the one we submitted, _____(16)_____ . _____(17)_____ combine their human needs with the needs of the operating system-not an easy task.

Next stages

_____(18)_____ work on three different areas of the project in order:

1. _____(19)_____ reorganize the data into new sets which are both more logical and easier for the system to manage. _____(20)_____ persuade them to go with our ideas on this, as this will then open up an opportunity for us to manage the system for them in the future, rather than leaving the management to their own engineer.

2. Once this is done, _____(21)_____ do the data retrieval systems. _____(22)_____ work out how to build growth capacity into the system, so that the system can grow as their customer base continues to expand.

3. _____(23)_____ (meet) the client at the end of next week to go through their needs for the interface.

In addition to these three future stages of the project, _____(24)_____

W o r d   L i s t

interface [ˋɪntəˌfes] *n.* 界面　　　　　retrieval [rɪˋtrivl] *n.* 恢復；取得

produce a training manual for the client, and ___(25)___ ensure that all their users receive training on the new system. This was not in the original proposal, but I hope I can persuade them to see the need for this and to increase the budget.

【報告摘要】

概要

　　專案如期進行，但有點超乎預算。雖然之前對方的 IT 經理持反對意見，但目前已漸漸培養出信任了，關係良好。

目前已經進行的

• 已組團隊討論如何符合客戶的需求，向他們提出提案，執行計畫也已底定。
• 已決定多安排兩名工程師，以利專案能如期完成，也可將專案進度讓他們知道。
• 取得客戶的資料庫，希望根據需求做最有效率的安排。

現階段

• 正由客戶資料發想出新方法以連結不同的資料群。
• 原有的資料貯存庫太小，目前正在建立一個新的資料庫。
• 新的連結運作不順暢仍在改善中。
• 客戶對我們提出的新介面不滿意，目前正試著將運作系統做更人性化的結合。

下一步

將依序進行專案中三個不同階段的工作。

1. 將資料以最符合邏輯以及最容易運作的方式重新編排，並說服對方採行，之後可有機會為他們進行系統的維護。
2. 取得資料庫，將多的空間納入系統中。
3. 下週末前與客戶碰面，瞭解他們對介面的需求。

除了上述三階段的計畫外，作客戶使用手冊，確保使用者都知道系統的使用方式。

答案 ▶

請看下列所提供的建議答案。有些空格的正確答案不只一個。選擇字串時,請考慮字串的意義並注意空格後面的文法。

1. We've already received
2. we've discussed
3. We've submitted
4. so that's done
5. has now been finalized
6. We've decided to
7. we've been able to
8. We've managed to
9. we've been able to
10. Right now we're in the middle of
11. we're in the process of
12. we've been building
13. we haven't finished
14. so that still needs more work
15. We're having problems
16. so that still needs to be done
17. We're trying to
18. We're going to
19. Our plan is to
20. Our intention is to
21. we're going to
22. We're taking steps to
23. I'm meeting
24. we're also making arrangements to
25. we're taking steps to

延伸寫作 ▶

請想一想目前手邊正在進行的專案。你已經達成了專案中的哪些任務,當下正在進行

哪些任務,未來還有哪些任務尚待完成?請作一個和前面的 Task 6.4 和 6.6 一樣的條列式筆記,然後利用筆記寫出一份專案進度報告。

 參考答案

以下提供一個範例。某超市為剛推出的忠誠卡 (loyalty card) 所寫的專案進度更新報告。

Supermarket Loyalty Card—Project Update

We've already designed the card, so that's ready to go. We've just sent the design to the manufacturer, and the number of units to be made has now been finalized. We've been able to get the individual franchise holders to agree to meet a share of the manufacturing cost. The card readers have also been made and are now ready to go.

We haven't yet worked out what percentage of the profits will go to the parent company, as this depends on what profits the loyalty program generates. However, right now we're in the middle of working out the math on this. We're also in the process of designing the software for collecting all the data the cards sent us. However, we are having problems agreeing on the categories, so that's not ready yet.

We're taking steps to increase awareness among consumers of the loyalty card program, and our plan is to introduce an attractive and high profile marketing campaign aimed at housewives. We've still got to agree on an advertising budget for the promotion. We intend to ask a celebrity to endorse the program, but we're still trying to agree on who this might be.

W o r d   L i s t

franchise [ˈfræn͵tʃaɪz] *n.* 特權;經銷權 (或公司名稱使用權等)
parent company 母公司

campaign [kæmˋpen] *n.* 活動
endorse [ɪnˋdɔrs] *v.* 贊同;認可

【報告摘要】

　　已將卡片樣式設計好，也寄送給製造商了，生產數量也已底定。個別的製造商同意共同分擔製造成本，讀卡機也已好了。

　　目前正試著計算母公司可分得的利潤有幾成，也正在設計資料收集的軟體，但對分類有不同的意見，因此正在協商中。

　　目前預計推出一項針對家庭主婦的行銷活動，打算找名人背書，不過對人選還未有共識。

　　好，本章的學習到此結束。請回到引言的「學習目標」，確定所有的項目都已確實了解了。

Unit 7

聯繫報告

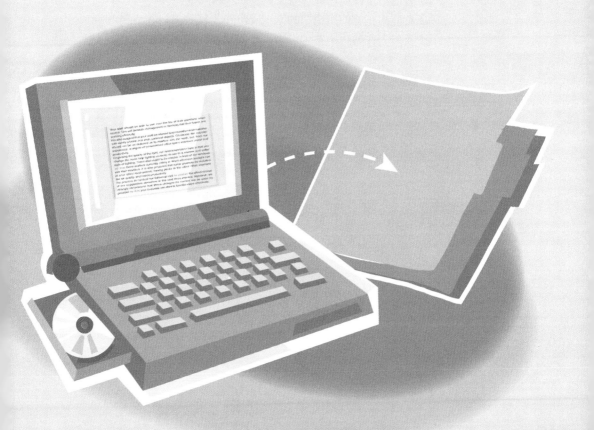

引言與學習目標

聯繫報告通常有兩種：會議報告和電話報告。會議報告為所有與會者提供了一份會議紀錄，也提供給有興趣的讀者，如股東或查帳員閱讀；電話報告基本上與會議報告大同小異，只是會議除了以電話會議的方式進行外，也可能以視訊會議的形式進行。會議報告和電話報告的用語其實相差不遠。

本章結束時，各位應達成的學習目標如下：

- ❑ 更清楚報告中應該放進哪些資訊。
- ❑ 了解報告的寫作過程。
- ❑ 有能力正確使用陳述意見的 verb chunks。
- ❑ 有能力正確使用總結的 verb chunks 和 word partnerships。
- ❑ 有能力在報告中寫出與會人士提出的問題和指示。

聯繫報告應具備的元素

我們就從研讀幾個會議報告和電話報告的範例開始。

TASK 7.1

請仔細閱讀下面兩份聯繫報告，列出兩者共同具備的元素。

會議報告

【背景說明】

　　Better 藥品有限公司是一間位於台灣的製藥商，專門生產專利權剛過期的藥（generic drugs），台灣政府近來對這類藥品的交易規範宣布了些許的改變。下列報告是由 Better 藥品公司的員工 Mike 所寫的。

Meeting Report

Date: December 11, 2004, 3:00 p.m.

Present: From Better Drugs, Inc.:

- Walter Chiou, CEO
- Joe Chen, New Product Development Manager
- Mike Lai, Marketing Executive

From the New Drugs Approval Bureau:

- Jonathan Chen, Assistant Under Minister for New Drugs
- Linda Liu, Deputy Assistant Under Minister for New Drugs

Location: New Drug Approval Bureau Office

Purpose: To discuss proposed new regulations for new drug approval

1. New regulations

W o r d   L i s t

present [ˈprɛzn̩t] *adj.* 出席的；列席的
executive [ɪgˈzɛkjutɪv] *n.* 執行者；經理；業務主管
bureau [ˈbjuro] *n.* （行政機構的）局

minister [ˈmɪnɪstə] *n.* 部長；大臣
deputy [ˈdɛpjətɪ] *n.* 代表；代理人

- Walter Chiou acknowledged receipt of the proposed new regulations. He voiced his concerns about them, and said that they are too restrictive. He explained that the additional amount of time needed to register new drugs will add unnecessary costs and will not be good for consumers who will have to wait for new treatments. He mentioned that the new regulations will also mean extensive changes to the procedures and staffing needs of local pharmaceutical companies. He also commented that it makes no sense for the Taiwanese government to impose such restrictions on drugs which have already been given approval in Europe and U.S. He also complained about the lack of communication between government bodies and major market players.
- Jonathan Chen outlined the plans for implementation of the new regulations. He argued that the new regulations are necessary because of the flood of generic drugs coming on to the market. He assured us that the new regulations will maintain consumer confidence. He stressed the need for establishing transparent quality controls in the market.

2. Consultation

- Jonathan announced that all the main players on the market, including Better Drugs, Inc. will be included in a consultancy exercise before the new regulations come into effect. This will give everyone a chance to air their views and for the final regulations to serve everyone's needs. He invited us to participate, and requested that we submit our ideas in writing and in detail before the consultation sessions begin in March.
- Walter inquired as to what other companies will also be invited to attend. Jonathan asked Linda to send us a complete list once other participants have been confirmed.

W o r d   L i s t

impose [ɪmˋpoz] *v.* 將（義務、負擔）加於人
body [ˋbɑdɪ] *n.* 組織；主體
player [ˋpleə] *n.* 參與者

transparent [ˋtræsˋpɛrənt] *adj.* 透明的
consultancy [kʌnˋsʌltənsɪ] *n.* 諮詢；顧問（工作）
air [ɛr] *v.* 發表；顯示

3. Follow-up
- Linda to send list of other participants by end of February
- Walter to prepare a detailed list of problems with the regulations by last week of February
- Linda to send details of consultation event, including date, time and location

【報告摘要】

會議目的：討論新法規對新藥核准的影響。

1. 新法規

- Walter 的意見：

他提出對新法規的疑慮，認為新法規太嚴苛，註冊新藥所花的時間會增加不必要的成本，而對等待新藥的消費者而言也不是好事。新法規也意味著程序以及製藥公司的雇員需求將有所改變。他更評論說台灣政府並無道理強加此項規範於此種已得到歐洲及美國政府核准的藥品。他更抱怨缺少溝通橋樑。

- Jonathan 的意見：

他已訂出執行新法規的計畫，並主張新法規是有必要的，此外，也向我們保證新法規可以維持消費者信心，更強調建立透明品管的需求。

2. 協商

- Jonathan 的意見：

他宣布包括 Better 藥品在內的市場上主要參與者，都將事前參與一協商會，他並邀請大家參加，事先將想法以書面方式呈現出來。

- Walter 詢問有哪些公司受邀參加，Jonathan 請 Linda 寄最後的確認名單給他。

3. 後續行動

- Linda 寄參與者的名單
- Walter 準備因新法規而有的問題
- Linda 寄協商會的詳細細節

電話報告

【背景說明】

　　Bonk 是一家位於台灣的數位錄音播放器製造商，他們正準備推出一個針對中國青少年市場的新 MP3 產品。他們近來和一家位於荷蘭阿姆斯特丹、叫做 Artful 的設計公司攜手合作。Bonk 的員工 Willy 紀錄了兩家公司的電話會議報告。

Conference Call Report

Date: December 12, 2004, 8:00 p.m.

Present: From Bonk:
- Oliver Lai, Senior Product Development Manager
- Willy Liu, Assistant to Oliver Lai

From Artful:
- Dirk Bogaerd, Senior Designer
- Bons Voirtrek, Senior Designer

Purpose: To discuss proposed designs for Impax007

1. Color
- Oliver raised the issue of the color. White is our preferred choice, but Dirk thinks this is too close to Apple's products, and he prefers black.
- Bons expressed her interest in using two colors and asked about our views on this. Oliver confirmed that he would like to see one color only.

2. Materials
- Bons reaffirmed her position on using shiny acrylic, although this is a more expensive material. She maintained that this will make the product look less like IBM's product, which uses matte black.
- Oliver admitted that some product differentiation is necessary in the design, but insisted that costs be kept down as much as possible.

 W o r d   L i s t

acrylic [æˋkrɪlɪk] *adj.* 【化】丙烯酸的；壓克力的　　　　matte [mæt] *adj.* 不反光的

- Dirk promised that they will try to find a shiny black acrylic which is also cheap. He enquired about plastics producers in Taiwan.

3. Style

- Dirk put forward a proposal for making the product round instead of square. He warned that this will add slightly to the cost, but claimed that it will make the product eye-catching and special. He estimated that it will increase the cost by 2%.
- Oliver instructed him to send a revised quotation for a round product.

4. Change of address for Artful

- Bons advised us to send all correspondence to their new email, given below.

5. Follow-up

- Willy to send Artful a list of plastics producers in Taiwan by the end of the week
- Artful to submit revised cost quotation for new design specs by Friday
- Artful to submit new designs, including revised shape and color by the end of the month

【報告摘要】

會議目的：討論 Impax007 的設計。

1. 顏色

- Oliver 認為白色是優先選擇，但 Dirk 認為白色跟 Apple 產品太像，因此他選黑色。
- Bons 覺得兩種顏色都使用也不錯，但 Oliver 確認說一種顏色即可。

2. 材質

- Bons 再次重申使用亮光壓克力的決心，以利產品跟 IBM 的可以有所區隔。
- Oliver 承認說產品在設計上的確需要有些不同，不過也堅持成本應降到最低。

enquire [ɪnˋkwaɪr] v. 詢問；查詢　　　　eye-catching [ˋaɪ͵kætʃɪŋ] adj. 引人注目的；顯著的

- Dirk 承諾會找到便宜的亮黑壓克力材質。

3. 樣式

- Dirk 提議略圓的產品，雖然成本會稍微增加，但產品會比較搶眼和特別。
- Oliver 指示 Dirk 送一份對此類產品的預估。

4. Artful 地址變更

- Bons 建議將所有通訊資料寄一份給他們。

5. 後續行動

- Willy 寄一份塑化製造業者的名單給 Artful
- Artful 提出修改後的成本預估
- Artful 提出新的設計樣式

答案 ▶

兩份報告共同具備的元素如下：

1. 聯繫的日期與時間、在場人士，以及若是面對面的會議，地點又是在哪兒。

2. 會議或通訊的目的均清楚地以 to V 表示。

3. 報告均按照開會前提出的議程為架構。

4. 報告均以條列的方式列出每個發言人所講的話，以利閱讀。

5. 以 to V 清楚地表示一些後續行動（follow-up），包括誰將主導追蹤行動，期限又是何時。

陳述意見的 verb chunks

我們已經學過聯繫報告中應該放入的資訊，現在就繼續往下學習這類報告的用語吧。第一個要注意的是時態。你可能已經注意到，閱讀報告時看到了很多陳述意見的 verb chunks。你可能也記得在學校時，曾經學過引述句或間接敘述句（reported speech）時態改變的複雜規則，其實真實世界中商業報告的寫作規則簡單得多了，這類的文法根本用不到。好消息一樁吧？我們就來看一看 Willy 和 Mike 是如何撰寫此類報告的。

Mike 首先根據當時講者使用的時態，記錄了會議中的討論內容，如下：

1. The new regulations are necessary because of the flood of generic drugs coming on to the market.
2. The new regulations will maintain consumer confidence.
3. It's necessary to establish transparent quality controls in the market.

接下來他使用了陳述意見的 verb chunks，如下列粗體字所示：

1. He **argued that** the new regulations are necessary because of the flood of generic drugs coming on to the market.
2. He **assured us that** the new regulations will maintain consumer confidence.
3. He **stressed the need for** establishing transparent quality controls in the market.

你會注意到兩份報告中引述別人的意見或看法的 verb chunks 都是簡單過去式，這是因為你報告的會議是屬於過去已經發生的事件。但報告事項的內容的動詞時態則和原來會議中使用的時態一致。我們回頭仔細看一下報告中出現過的所有動詞。

TASK 7.2

請再看一次 Task 7.1 的兩份報告，找出所有的過去式動詞，並劃底線。做這個練習的

時候，思考一下剛剛學過的東西。

答案 ▶

希望做完這個 Task 之後，你對報告的哪些部分必須用簡單過去式、哪些部分不需用簡單過去式有更清楚的了解。

現在我們來進一步研讀這些陳述意見的 verb chunks 吧。我們將根據這些 verb chunks 的功能和意義做分類。

TASK 7.3

研讀下列語庫，哪些 verb chunks 在 Task 7.1 的報告中出現過？用法為何？

提案 必備語庫 7.1 ▶　　(後面接 that + n. clause 的 verb chunks)

• acknowledged that + n. clause	認知到
• admitted that + n. clause	承認了
• agreed that + n. clause	同意了
• announced that + n. clause	宣布了
• answered that + n. clause	答覆了
• argued that + n. clause	主張要
• assured sb. that + n. clause	向某人保証要……
• claimed that + n. clause	主張要
• commented that + n. clause	評論說
• confirmed that + n. clause	證實了
• denied that + n. clause	否定了
• estimated that + n. clause	估計了
• explained that + n. clause	解釋說
• informed sb. that + n. clause	告知說
• insisted that + n. clause	堅持要
• maintained that + n. clause	主張要
• mentioned that + n. clause	提到了
• promised that + n. clause	保証說
• recommended that + n. clause	建議要
• replied that + n. clause	回覆了

• reported that + n. clause	報告說
• requested that + n. clause	要求說
• suggested that + n. clause	提議了
• threatened that + n. clause	威脅要
• warned that + n. clause	警告說

★ 📁 語庫小叮嚀

◆ 在聯繫報告中使用這些動詞時，永遠記得要使用簡單過去式。

◆ 有的 verb chunks 在 that 前面會有一個受詞 (sb.)。你可以根據參與人數決定要用單數還是複數，例如 me 或 us。

　　我想你會發現這些動詞不難運用，唯一會讓你覺得難度有點高的地方，可能是將動詞連結到正確的上下文情境中。請做下面的 Task，克服這個問題。

TASK 7.4

請將下列 comments 中的句子與適當的 verb chunks 配對，並將它們組成完整的句子。有的句子可和多個 verb chunks 配對。請看範例 1。

Verb Chunks	Comments
1. acknowledged that + n. clause	a) According to our research, the yellow model is more popular.
2. agreed that + n. clause	b) I agree with you that we should postpone the start.
3. answered that + n. clause	c) I think you should choose the latest model.
4. confirmed that + n. clause	d) If you don't lower your prices, we will look for another supplier.
5. denied that + n. clause	e) No, that's not true. We are not going to look for another supplier.
6. informed sb. that + n. clause	f) To answer your question, I don't think it's possible to go ahead now.
7. recommended that + n. clause	g) We are definitely going to open a new store.
8. replied that + n. clause	h) Well yes, I suppose you are right. We did make a mistake.
9. reported that + n. clause	
10. suggested that + n. clause	
11. threatened that + n. clause	

___h___ **1.** *He acknowledged that they made a mistake.*

___ **2.** _____

___ **3.** _____

___ **4.** _____

___ **5.** _____

___ **6.** _____

___ **7.** _____

___ **8.** _____

___ **9.** _____

___ **10.** _____

___ **11.** _____

答案▶

___b___ **2.** He agreed that we should postpone the start.

___f___ **3.** He answered that he doesn't think it's possible to go ahead now.

___g___ **4.** He confirmed that they are going to open a new store.

___e___ **5.** He denied that they are going to look for another supplier.

___g___ **6.** He informed us that they are going to open a new store.

___c___ **7.** He recommended that we choose the latest model.

___f___ **8.** He replied that he doesn't think it's possible to go ahead now.

___a___ **9.** He reported that the yellow model is more popular.

___c___ **10.** He suggested that we choose the latest model.

___d___ **11.** He threatened that they will look for another supplier.

★🗀 語庫小叮嚀

◆ 請注意，只有重複或引述別人意見的 verb chunks 是用簡單過去式，其他的如原 comments 一樣維持原本的時態即可，因為除非句子裡有明確的時間 chunks，否則我們無從得知子句裡指的是過去還是現在的事情。

◆ 若使用 denied 來改寫句子，後面所接的子句應該使用肯定句，意即無需再加 not，因為 denied 本身已帶有否定的意思。

◆ 還記得嗎？Recommend 跟 suggest 後面的子句所接的動詞要記得用原形。

剛才學過的一些動詞中，有些可以跟 n.p. 一起用，不一定非得用 n. clause 不可。當這些 verb chunks 和 n.p. 一起使用時，可用來概述先前說過的事情。舉個例子：

+ n. clause ： He suggested that we choose the latest model.
+ n.p. ： He suggested the latest model.

相信這個概念不難理解，現在就跟我們來研讀此種用法吧。

TASK 7.5

請研讀下列語庫。哪些 verb chunks 在 Task 7.1 的報告中出現過？用法為何？

提案 必備語庫 7.2 ▶ (後面接 n.p. 的 verb chunks)

- complained about n.p.
- agreed about n.p.
- explained (about) n.p.
- warned us about n.p.

TASK 7.6

請將下列 comments 與適當的 verb chunks 配對，同樣地，將之改寫為完整句子，請看範例。

Verb Chunks	Comments
1. complained about n.p.	a) I agree with you that we need to look for a new distributor.
2. agreed about n.p.	b) Let me explain why the heat disperser is not functioning properly at the moment.
3. explained (about) n.p.	c) We are really not very happy with the service we've been getting from you recently.
4. warned us about n.p.	d) I think it's possible that your main competitor might attempt a hostile takeover.

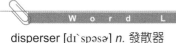 W o r d   L i s t

disperser [dɪ`spɝsə] *n.* 發散器      takeover [`tek͵ovə] *n.* 接收；接管；收購

___c___ **1.** *He complained about our service.* _____

_____ **2.** _____

_____ **3.** _____

_____ **4.** _____

答案 ▶

以下是我的建議答案，每個用語可組合成多個不同的句子。

___a___ **2.** We agreed about the need for a new distributor.

___b___ **3.** He explained (about) the problem with the heat disperser.

___d___ **4.** He warned us about the possibility of a hostile takeover bid.

傳達問題／指示的 verb chunks

　　開會時與會人士常會提出建議、指示或者問題。我們這就來學習如何在報告中寫出這類評語。

TASK 7.7

請研讀下列語庫。哪些 verb chunks 在 Task 7.1 的報告中出現過？用法為何？

提案 必備語庫 7.3

Question Reporting Verbs (傳達問題的動詞)	Instruction Reporting Verbs (傳達指示的動詞)
• asked (sb.) wh- + n. clause • asked about n.p. • inquired (as to) wh- + n. clause • inquired about n.p.	• advised sb. to V • asked sb. to V • instructed sb. to V • invited sb. to V • warned sb. to V

★ 語庫小叮嚀

◆ 敘述與會者提出的問題時，應該使用 asked (sb.) wh- + n. clause 和 asked about n.p.。若是敘述與會者提出的要求時，則應該使用 asked sb. to V。

TASK 7.8

請將 comments 與適當的 verb chunks 配對，並將它們組合成完整句。有的 comments 可和多個 verb chunks 配對。請看範例。

Verb Chunks	**Comments**
1. asked (sb.) wh- + n. clause	**a)** Be very careful about your raw materials storage.
2. asked about n.p.	**b)** Do you think you could give us a discount?
3. asked sb. to V	
4. inquired (as to) wh- + n. clause	**c)** I would advise you to lower your prices.
5. inquired about n.p.	**d)** I'd be delighted if you could attend my retirement party on Saturday.
6. advised sb. to V	**e)** What's happening about the Impax 007 project?
7. instructed sb. to V	
8. invited sb. to V	**f)** Why has it been delayed?
9. warned sb. to V	**g)** You must keep better transaction records.

_____f_____ **1.** *He asked why it has been delayed.*

_____ **2.** _____

_____ **3.** _____

_____ **4.** _____

_____ **5.** _____

_____ **6.** _____

_____ **7.** _____

_____ **8.** _____

_____ **9.** _____

答案 ▶

以下提供我的參考答案。

_____e_____ **2.** He asked about the Impax007 project.

_____b_____ **3.** He asked us to give him a discount.

_____f_____ **4.** He inquired as to why it has been delayed.

_____e_____ **5.** He inquired about the Impax007 project.

_____c_____ **6.** He advised us to lower our prices.

_____g_____ **7.** He instructed us to keep better transaction records.

_____d_____ **8.** He invited us to attend his retirement party on Saturday.

_____a_____ **9.** He warned us to be very careful about raw materials storage.

W o r d   L i s t

160   raw material 原物料　　transaction [træn`zækʃən] *n.* 交易；辦理

簡單概述某議題的 verb chunks

現在我要教你本章中最後一組動詞，這組語庫是由動詞和名詞組合而成。需要簡潔扼要地概述大量的討論內容時，這些字串特別有用。

TASK 7.9

請研讀下列語庫。哪些用語在 Task 7.1 的報告中出現過？用法為何？

報告 必備語庫 7.4

• acknowledged receipt of n.p.	• raised the issue of n.p.
• expressed an interest in n.p.	• reaffirmed sb.'s position on n.p.
• outlined the plans for n.p.	• stressed the importance of n.p.
• put forward a proposal for n.p.	• voiced sb.'s concerns about n.p.
• put forward a proposal to V	
• questioned the need for n.p.	

TASK 7.10

請閱讀下列文字，並從語庫 7.4 中選出適當的 verb chunks 來概述下列文字。請看範例。

例句

1. I would like to propose a change of distributor for the following reasons: (1) we need to save money, (2) we have had complaints from customers about the inefficiency of the current distributor, and (3) they also lack growth capacity, which we will be needing in the coming months.

   He put forward a proposal to change our distributor.

2. I'm very worried about the strategy for the new product line, for a number of reasons. First, I think it doesn't take into account the strength of our competitors in this area. Secondly, I think as the strategy stands, we have not allocated enough budget to it.

---

3. Do we really need DMs and printouts? I mean, do we really know exactly how effective these measures are in terms of advertising reach? I think most people put them straight into the bin.

答案 ▶

以下為我的建議答案。希望你看得出來，只要使用這些 verb chunks，即可簡明扼要地概述大量原始的討論內容。

2. He voiced his concerns about the new product line strategy.
3. He questioned the need for DMs and printouts.

好，本章中聯繫報告的學習到此結束。在繼續學習下一章之前，請做下面的延伸寫作題，鞏固在本章中學到的知識。

延伸寫作 ▶

請錄下與某人的一段對話，然後利用在本章學過的用語寫一份報告，描述這段對話。

參考答案 ▶

下頁提供我的答案讓你參考。

 W o r d   L i s t

printout [ˋprɪnt͵aʊt] *n.* 印製物　　　　　　bin [bɪn] *n.* 垃圾桶

Annual Job Appraisal Meeting

Roger began by asking me whether I was happy in my first year with the company. I assured him that I was. He then raised the issue of the problem with XYZ client and inquired as to what I was planning to do about it. I promised that I was trying to solve it, but he commented that the customer was very angry with us. I acknowledged that it was my mistake, and reported that I was making good progress in rebuilding good relations with the client. He advised me to be careful in the future to avoid making the same mistake. I then inquired about a pay increase for the next year, but he gave me a funny look, and explained that my mistake had already cost the company quite a lot of money. Then he informed me that there would be no pay raise for me next year.

【報告摘要】

Roger 詢問我在公司的第一年是否開心,接著提出了跟 XYZ 客戶間的議題,並問我打算要怎麼做。我知道這是我的錯,也保證我會盡力解決,盡力重建與客戶間的關係。他也建議我以後要小心點避免再出錯,我接著詢問關於加薪事宜。不過卻慘遭白眼,他說我造成的錯誤已讓公司賠了很多錢,明年要加薪是無望了。

好啦!總算進入本章尾聲,記得盡量在下一次的眞實會議或電話報告中運用這些用語,若能反覆不斷地練習,相信你的寫作功力一定會更加進步的。

W o r d   L i s t

appraisal [ə`prezl] *n.* 評價;評鑑

Unit 8
財務報告

引言與學習目標

　　所有的商業報告均包含財務的相關資訊，而且經常利用表格、圖表、曲線圖和其他種類的圖示以視覺輔助的方式呈現，不過，若能使用文字特別解說部分圖示，強調某產品的性能或某個業務代表的業績，甚至某個地區的業績成長，往往也能收得良效。解說圖示的時候，請務必注意文字和視覺圖示必須百分之百吻合，否則讀者會看得糊里糊塗，納悶：到底文字敘述跟視覺圖示哪一個是正確的？在讀者尋找答案的時候，很可能就對你失去了信心，你可不希望有這樣的結果吧？！因此在本章中，我將教你描述財務圖示的字串。在一些細微但很重要的地方所使用的文字得高度準確，這可不簡單。本章篇幅很長，我建議你將學習速度放慢，並分段學習。

　　在本章中我們要學習財務報告的六大元素，如下：

- 數字變化 (movement)
- 數據 (figures)
- 時間 (time)
- 引述 (reporting)
- 比較 (comparing)
- 原因和結果 (reason and result)

　　本章結束時，各位應達成的「學習目標」如下：

- ☐ 對財務報告的六大元素有更深入的瞭解。
- ☐ 有能力以文字描述銷售、成本、利潤和其他指標。
- ☐ 有能力在報告中準確的使用數據和正確的時間 chunks。
- ☐ 更能掌握隱含或內顯的比較，並有效運用這些比較結果。
- ☐ 有能力引述和說明數字變化的原因和結果。
- ☐ 能夠更精確的理解財務報告。

首先我們來看一個範例。

TASK 8.1

請閱讀下面的報告和表格，同時找出我先前提過的六大元素。

【背景說明】

　　UBP 是一家塑膠衛浴用品的製造商和外銷公司，市場遍及歐洲、亞洲和美國，股票已在台灣上市。下面是該公司的財務部主管寫給股東的年度表現報告，旨在比較亞洲地區今年與去年的銷售成績和所花的成本，共分兩段。這份報告寫於第四季。

> 　　Sales in the Asian Region picked up dramatically in the first quarter of last year, largely due to the fact that a new product was launched. Sales managers said that it proved extremely popular with the youth segment, accounting for the sale of an additional 35,000 units. At the same time, the increased production meant that costs also saw a rise from NT$150 million to NT$250 million. In the second quarter while sales still went up, they increased less quickly. Costs also rose slightly owing to the increase in the price of crude oil. In quarter three the arrival of a foreign product similar to ours meant that sales began to fall. Costs remained steady at just over NT$300 million. This situation continued in Q4, with sales suffering a downward trend to close at 52,000 units, up 32,000 units from the same time a year earlier.
>
> 　　This year saw a steady decline in sales in the first half of the year. Production costs stayed the same at NT$310 million during this peri-

Word List

owing to　由於……

crude [krud] *adj.* 天然的；未經加工的

Q (=quarter) [ˋkwɔrtə] *n.* 一季

od. At the end of Q2 we increased our advertising budget and developed a major new campaign aimed at the slightly older segment of the market. As a result, sales grew again by a few thousand units in the later half of Q3. At the same time, our cost cutting drive implemented in March began to show results, with factory managers reporting a fall in costs to just under $250 million starting in Q3.

【報告摘要】

　　亞洲區的銷售在去年第一季有大幅度的成長，主要是因為新商品的推出，新商品很受年輕族群的歡迎，讓銷售數量額外增加了三萬五千個，在此同時，成本也從原本的一千五百萬增加到兩千一百萬。第二季時，雖然銷售仍在增長，卻增加的沒那麼快速了，此時的成本卻因為原油的上漲而微幅上揚。到了第三季，由於有外國新商品加入戰場，意味著銷售會開始下跌，成本維持在三千多萬的情況一直持續到第四季，此時銷售卻下降，數量僅有五萬兩千個，但跟去年同期相比卻增加了三萬兩千個。

　　今年上半，銷售仍持續下跌。成本卻維持不變，第二季末，增加了廣告預算，並發想了一個針對年長稍長族群的活動，因此銷售在第三季末出現了稍微的增長，成本刪減也開始出現了成果，從第三季開始，成本就已經降至兩千五百萬元以下。

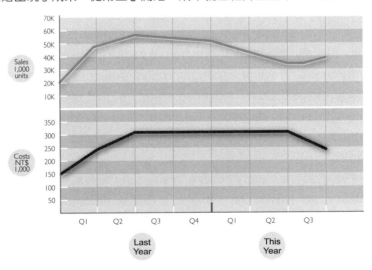

drive [draɪv] *n.* (為達到某目的的) 運動／活動

答案 ▶

你在本章結束前還會再做一次這個 Task，到時可以看出自己進步的程度。現在我們先
來一一學習前面提到的六大元素。

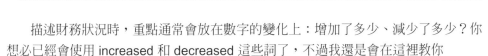

數字變化

描述財務狀況時，重點通常會放在數字的變化上：增加了多少、減少了多少？你想必已經會使用 increased 和 decreased 這些詞了，不過我還是會在這裡教你

財務報告中其他經常用來描述數字變化的動詞。

TASK 8.2

請將下面的 chunks 分類，寫在表格中

1. ... closed up ...	**13.** ... dipped ...	**25.** ... snapped back ...
2. ... decreased ...	**14.** ... dropped ...	**26.** ... stabilized ...
3. ... gained ...	**15.** ... fell ...	**27.** ... stayed the same ...
4. ... increased ...	**16.** ... fluctuated ...	**28.** ... troughed ...
5. ... jumped ...	**17.** ... held steady ...	**29.** ... went down ...
6. ... peaked ...	**18.** ... plummeted ...	**30.** ... went up ...
7. ... picked up ...	**19.** ... recovered ...	**31.** ... withered ...
8. ... rallied ...	**20.** ... remained steady ...	**32.** ... plunged ...
9. ... rose ...	**21.** ... shot up ...	**33.** ... hovered around ...
10. ... soared ...	**22.** ... shrank ...	**34.** ... closed down ...
11. ... bounced back ...	**23.** ... grew ...	
12. ... declined ...	**24.** ... stagnated ...	

Movement Up	Movement Down	Very Little Movement

rally [ˋrælɪ] v. 集合；重整

fluctuate [ˋflʌktʃʊ͵et] v. 波動

shrink [ʃrɪŋk] v. 退縮；迴避

stagnate [ˋstægnet] v. 腐敗；蕭條

trough [trɔf] n. 低谷；蕭條階段（此處當動詞用）

wither [ˋwɪðɚ] v. 衰弱；減弱

答案▶

請利用下面的表格核對答案，並研讀語庫小叮嚀。

報告 必備語庫 8.1　　　（描述數字變化的 chunks）

Movement Up（數字上升）	Movement Down（數字下降）	Very Little Movement（數字變化不大）
• … closed up … • … gained … • … jumped … • … rallied … • … picked up … • … rose … • … soared … • … bounced back … • … recovered … • … shot up … • … went up … • … snapped back … • … increased … • … grew …	• … closed down … • … declined … • … dipped … • … dropped … • … fell … • … shrank … • … went down … • … withered … • … decreased … • … plunged … • … plummeted …	• … held steady … • … peaked … • … stabilized … • … troughed … • … stayed the same … • … remained steady … • … fluctuated … • … stagnated … • … hovered around …

★🗀 **語庫小叮嚀**

◆ 請注意，這些動詞都是簡單過去式，這是因為財務報告中描述的時間通常都是已經結束的，也因此才能得到可用的數據。不過記住，如果要描述較長，且尚未結束的時間，如 this year，則必須改用現在完成式。倘若你對時態的用法還不是很清楚，請再回頭複習一次第二章。

◆ Closed up 和 closed down 是用來描述某段時期終了時的情況，如 At the end of trading, stocks closed down.。

◆ Rallied、bounced back、snapped back 和 recovered 等詞可用來描述數字回復到先前情況的現象，具有正面意義。這些詞可用來描述增長中的數字、也可以用來描述減少中的數字，雖然前者比較常見，但如果描寫的是成本或債務等資訊，圖示則會顯示出下滑中的數字。

◆ Shot up 是上升得非常快的意思，soared 則是指飆高。
◆ Withered 和 shrank 可用來描述數字微幅的下滑；dipped 則是用來描述數字原本下滑了，但緊接著卻又上揚了。
◆ Peaked 在字面上是山頂的意思，可用來描述數字達到最高點的時候，也就是數字不再上升而準備開始下滑的情況；troughed 則剛好相反，它描述的是數字停止下滑、準備開始上揚了。
◆ Fluctuated 被歸類在表格中「變化幅度不大」一欄裡，但它描述的其實是數字起起伏伏的狀況，請看例句：
Both political instability and natural disasters can cause oil prices to fluctuate wildly.

TASK 8.3

請挑選六個動詞 chunks，造出六個句子來描述 Task 8.1 圖表中的一些數字變化。

答案▶

下面提供六個參考答案，大部分是很多人不知道如何使用的動詞。

1. Sales rallied in Q1 of last year.
2. Costs held steady for the much of year.
3. Production costs shrank in Q3.
4. Sales peaked at the end of Q2.
5. Costs have withered so far this year.
6. Sales declined in the first half.

　　這些動詞有許多也可當作名詞使用，用來描述數據曲線，如果還不是很瞭解我的意思，請繼續往下研讀，你會更明白。

TASK 8.4

請將這些用語分類，填入下表中。

1. … a decrease (of X) in Y …
2. … a downward trend in Y …
3. … a dramatic downturn in Y …
4. … a fall (of X) in Y …
5. … a gain (of X) in Y …
6. … a loss (of X) in Y …
7. … a peak in Y …
8. … a record high (of X) in Y …
9. … a record low (of X) in Y …
10. … a recovery in Y …
11. … a rise (of X) in Y …
12. … a slump in Y …
13. … a steady decline in Y …
14. … a trend downwards in Y …
15. … a trend upwards in Y …
16. … a trough in Y …
17. … an all-time high (of X) in Y
18. … an all-time low in Y …
19. … an increase (of X) in Y …
20. … an upward trend in Y …
21. … some signs of growth in Y.
22. … some signs of recovery in Y …

Movement Up	Movement Down

recovery [rɪˋkʌvərɪ] *n.* 重獲；復甦

答案 ▶

請利用下面的語庫核對答案,並研讀語庫小叮嚀。

報告 必備語庫 8.2 ▶ (描述數字變化的 chunks)

Movement Up(數字上升)	Movement Down(數字下降)
• … a gain (of X) in Y …	• … a dramatic downturn in Y …
• … some signs of growth in Y…	• … an all-time low in Y …
• … a recovery in Y …	• … a decrease (of X) in Y …
• … a trend upwards in Y …	• … a fall (of X) in Y …
• … an upward trend in Y …	• … a record low (of X) in Y …
• … some signs of recovery in Y …	• … a slump in Y …
• … a record high (of X) in Y …	• … a downward trend in Y …
• … an all-time high (of X) in Y …	• … a trend downwards in Y …
• … an increase (of X) in Y …	• … a loss (of X) in Y …
• … a rise (of X) in Y …	• … a trough in Y …
• … a peak in Y …	• … a steady decline in Y …

★ 語庫小叮嚀

◆ 許多名詞的後面接的是 of X in Y 或 in Y 等 chunks。X 代表數字;Y 則代表一個主題或一段時期,如 … a rise of 2% in costs 或 … a rise of 2% in Q2。

◆ 雖然有些名詞可列於「數字變化不大」一欄內,如 peak、stabilization、trough、 fluctuation、stagnation,但如果需要描述此類情況,還是建議使用動詞會比較好。

◆ 通常這些名詞片語(record high / loss)會跟下列這四個動詞一起連用:enjoyed(描述有正面意涵的曲線)、suffered(描述有負面意涵的曲線)、saw / There was …(兩個正負面都可以用),請看以下範例:

1. There was a loss of 5% in market share.

   Market share saw a loss of 5%.

   Market share suffered a loss of 5%.

2. There was a record high of 9,637 units in sales.

Sales saw a record high of 9,637 units.

Sales enjoyed a record high of 9,637 units.

請注意這些例句中語氣的改變。

好,現在我們就來練習使用這些 chunks 吧。

TASK 8.5

請從語庫 8.2 中挑出適當的用語,配合上述我教你的四個連用的動詞,改寫你在 Task 8.3 中所寫的句子,但大致上維持原意。請看範例。

1. Sales rallied in Q1 of last year.

   There was a recovery in sales in Q1 of last year.

2. _____

3. _____

4. _____

5. _____

6. _____

答案 ▶

以下提供我的參考答案,請注意句中的詞類變化,並與我為 Task 8.2 所寫的答案做比較。

2. Costs held steady for much of the year.

   同上句 (用動詞來描述數字變化不大的情況)

3. Production costs shrank in Q3.

   Production costs saw a fall in Q3.

4. Sales peaked at the end of Q2.

   There was a peak in sales at the end of Q2.

5. Costs have withered so far this year.
   <u>Costs have enjoyed a downward trend so far this year.</u>

6. Sales declined in the first half.
   <u>Sales suffered a slump in the first half.</u>

　　好，在我們繼續研讀下一個元素之前，請再做一個 Task，鞏固目前已經學到的用語。

TASK 8.6

請閱讀下面描述歐洲股市的報告，並在已學過的動詞或名詞 chunks 下畫底線。

European Markets Roundup

European markets saw an upward trend across the board Monday after the holiday break. In Frankfurt the DAX index recovered after its poor showing last week, when shares rallied 1.6% to 3,379 just before closing. In Milan, prices held steady despite poor fourth quarter figures. Lisbon suffered a slump in trading volume, which was not balanced by a gain in shipping stocks. In Paris, the CAC-40 bounced back slightly, finishing up by 0.9% to end at 3,167, while in London the FTSE suffered a loss of 0.7% in early trading, but snapped back to close at 4,989.80 just before the bell.

請核對你的答案，並閱讀報告摘要。

European Markets Roundup

European markets <u>saw an upward trend</u> across the board Monday after the holiday break. In Frankfurt the DAX index <u>recovered</u>

---

after its poor showing last week, when shares <u>rallied</u> 1.6% to 3,379 just before closing. In Milan, prices <u>held steady</u> despite poor fourth quarter figures. Lisbon <u>suffered a slump in trading volume</u>, which was not balanced by <u>a gain in shipping stocks</u>. In Paris, the CAC-40 <u>bounced back</u> slightly, finishing up by 0.9% to end at 3,167, while in London the FTSE <u>suffered a loss of 0.7% in early trading</u>, but <u>snapped back</u> to close at 4,989.80 just before the bell.

【報告摘要】

　　禮拜一一開盤，歐洲股市全體均呈現上揚的趨勢。法蘭克福的 DAX 指數在上週表現疲乏後，終於止跌回升，上漲了一點六個百分點，指數來到了 3,379 點。在米蘭，儘管第四季的表現不佳，指數仍維持平盤。里斯本的交易量則呈現下滑，並沒有因航運股的上漲而獲利。巴黎的 CAC-40 稍微回升了一些，上漲了零點九個百分點，收在 3,167 點。倫敦的 FSTE 指數在稍早下跌了零點七個百分點，但在休市的前一刻，卻又回升到 4989.80 點。

TASK 8.7

現在請把報告中的動詞改為名詞、名詞改為動詞，重新寫一篇報告，但請維持原意。

答案

請參考我在下面提供的版本，並與自己寫的版本和原版作比較，修改過的地方以粗體表示。

European Markets Roundup

　　European markets **gained** across the board on Monday after the holiday break. In Frankfurt the DAX index **saw some signs of recovery** after its poor showing last week, when shares **enjoyed an increase of 1.6%** to 3,379 just before closing. In Milan, prices **stabilized** despite poor fourth quarter figures. Trading volume in Lisbon **shrank** despite the fact that shipping stocks **rose**. In Paris, **there was**

a slight recovery in the CAC-40, finishing up by 0.9% to end at 3,167 while in London the FTSE **dipped** by 0.7% in early trading, but **enjoyed a recovery** to close at 4,989.80 just before the bell.

數據

　　寫報告時覺得描述數字很難的原因，通常在於不知該如何結合語言和數字本身，這是因為數字有兩種：代表差距（distance）的數字，如 Sales rose by 3,000 units.，還有代表數字起迄點（point）的數字，如Sales rose from 12,000 to 15,000 units.。這時你用的介系詞，就可顯示出數字指的是 distance 還是 point。因此若是介系詞用錯，數字的意思便會隨之改變。這是報告裡，文字和數字結合時無法避免的主要問題，也是造成錯誤的主要原因。寫報告時你應該要非常仔細，小心避免這種問題。

TASK 8.8

請回頭再次閱讀 Task 8.6 中的報告，並在數字下面畫底線。這些數字代表的是 point 還是 distance？你怎麼看出來的呢？

答案▶

請用下面的語庫核對答案，並研讀語庫小叮嚀。

報告 必備語庫 8.3 ▶　（描述數字的 chunks）

Distance（差距）	Point（起迄點）
• … X points/units … • … X percent/% … • … (by) X points/units … • … (by) X percent/% … • … from X to Z … • … of X % … • … of X points/units …	• … to X … • … from X … • … to end at X … • … to close at X … • … be at X … • … at X …

★ 🗁 語庫小叮嚀

◆ 一般而言在描寫 distance 的時候，數字要寫在文字的前面（除了 of 以外）。描寫 point 的時候，數字則要寫在文字的後面。

◆ 請注意，兩個 point chunks 可以組合在一起，如 from X to Z，變成一個 distance chunk。

◆ 寫百分比的時候，可以用百分比的符號 (%)，也可以拼出來，如 percent。兩者同樣正確，但請注意同一份報告中要維持一致。

◆ 如果報告中 point 和 distance 都得描述，應先描述 distance。

TASK 8.9

請寫出六個句子，描述 Task 8.1 圖表中的數字。請看範例。

1. *Sales rallied by 36,000 units in Q1 of last year.*
2. _____
3. _____
4. _____
5. _____
6. _____

答案▶

以下提供我的參考答案。

2. Production costs saw a fall of 22.58% in Q3.
3. Sales declined from 51,000 to 34,000 units in the first half.
4. Sales peaked at 65,000 units at the end of Q2.
5. Sales saw a slump of 34.62% in the first half.
6. Costs have enjoyed a downward trend of 70,000 so far this year, to close at 240,000.

時間

　　財務報告的第三個元素就是時間用語。我在第二章所教的時間 chunks，大部分都可適用於本章中，因此在繼續往下學習之前，你可以回去複習一下之前做過的 Task。比起其他用語，時間用語非常直接了當，但務必表達清楚你所指的時間範圍，時間 chunks 也得吻合動詞時態的意義。我在下面的語庫中，提供了財務報告最常用到的，而且也非常有用的時間 chunks。

TASK 8.10

請將下面語庫中的用語分類。類別可自由決定。

報告 必備語庫 8.4 ▶　(財務報告的時間 chunks)

• in the last quarter (of the year)	• in the second half (of the year)
• at the end of Q2	• this quarter
• in the first quarter (of the year)	• at the end of the year
• this year	• in Q4
• in the previous quarter	• last quarter
• last year	• in Q4 of last year
• in 1999	• in Q1 of this year
• in March	• at the beginning of the year
• in the same period	• in the later half of the year
• at the same time	• at the beginning of Q2
• in the first half (of the year)	• in the early half of the year

答案 ▶

你可以根據 in 或 at 將這些用語分門別類。不管以何種方法分類，請將這些 chunks 中的所有小字，如 the 和 of 都記起來。

現在請再做一個 Task，練習如何使用這些時間 chunks 來造句。

TASK 8.11

在下表中，我分別從語庫 8.2 跟 8.4 裡選出了一些 MWIs，請將表格的兩邊結合起來，造出完整的句子，請見範例。

1. … some signs of growth in Y …	in Q4
2. … a dramatic downturn in Y …	at the end of the year
3. … an upward trend in Y …	this quarter
4. … a loss (of X) in Y …	last year
5. … a recovery in Y …	in the later half of the year
6. … an all-time low in Y … / … a record high (of X) in Y	at the same time

例句 ▶

1. Sales showed some signs of growth in Q4.

答案 ▶

以下提供我的參考答案。

2. We saw a dramatic downturn in mergers and acquisitions at the end of the year.
3. There has been an upward trend in our stock price this quarter.
4. We suffered a loss of NT$83 million last year.
5. The local economy experienced a recovery in the later half of the year.
6. We had an all-time low in sales and a record high in costs at the same time.

現在我們要繼續往下學習下一個元素，也就是引述用語。

acquisition [ˌækwəˈzɪʃən] *n.* 購併；收購

引述用語

做財務報告時，有時會有必要告知讀者數字或資訊的來源，這時便需要使用類似第七章裡的引述動詞。不過比起電話報告，財務報告中用到的引述動詞種類少得多，因此不用花太多時間便可輕鬆學會！

TASK 8.12

請研讀下面財務報告中會出現的引述動詞。

報告 必備語庫 8.5 ▶ (引述的 chunks)

• … said + n. clause … • … reiterated + n. clause … • … reported + n. clause … • … posted n.p. … • … reiterated n.p. … • … reported n.p. …	• … warned + n. clause … • … warned about n.p. … • … attributed the increase to n.p. … • … announced + n. clause… • … agreed + n. clause … • … announced n.p. …

★ 📁 語庫小叮嚀

◆ 請注意，這些動詞大部分都是簡單過去式。這就像描述數字變化的動詞一樣，我們通常要引述的是某人過去說過的事。

◆ 大部分的行業中，最常用到的兩個引述動詞就是 said 和 reported。不過金融業的報告用的動詞種類較為繁複。現在我們就來看一下幾個範例吧。

Word List

reiterate [riˋɪtəˏret] v. 重申；反覆做　　　　post [post] v. 宣布

TASK 8.13

請閱讀下面的報告，在引述動詞下畫底線。請參考語庫 8.5，注意引述動詞的用法。

【背景說明】

全球財富管理公司是一家位於上海的小型個人財務投資事務所，專門為國際客戶管理私人財務，並提供私人理財方面的顧問服務。他們每個月會為客戶提供英文報告，說明客戶投資組合裡各公司的財務狀況。

Research in Movement (RMM: up $3.26 to $272.94) S&P reiterated a "market outperform" on the stock, saying that negative corporate news has already been priced into the share price.

Nuke (NKE: up $5.12 to $30.65) The world's largest maker of athletic shoe and clothing announced after the market closed on Thursday that it expected modest earnings and revenue growth for the rest of its fiscal year as it remains cautious about the U.S. retail environment.

Immuno (BLDD: up $1.53 to $50.10) The manufacturer of blood transfusion machinery reported a profit for its fiscal second quarter, compared with a loss in the same period a year ago. The company posted a net income of $1.8 million, or 45 cents per diluted share, for the period ended June 30.

Shirley & Roger (CHBS: up $3.38 to $36.23) The women's apparel retailer announced a 29 percent rise in fiscal fourth-quarter

---

W o r d   L i s t

athletic [æθˋlɛtɪk] *adj.* 體育的；運動的
fiscal [ˋfɪskl] *adj.* 財政的；會計的
transfusion [trænsˋfjuʒən] *n.* 輸液；輸血

diluted [daɪˋlutɪd] *adj.* 稀釋的
apparel [əˋpærəl] *n.* 服裝；衣著

earnings, helped by strong sales at the company's newer stores. However, the company warned that it expects sales at stores which have already been open for at least a year——or same-store sales—— to fall well below its previously stated forecast for growth of 7 percent.

【報告摘要】

Research in Movement (股票代號：RMM，上漲了3.26 點，來到 272.94 點)
標準普爾指數重申市場股價表現超乎預期，也就是負面的企業新聞已經被股價弭平。

Nuke (股票代號：NKE，上漲了 5.12 點，來到 30.65 點)
市場上最大的運動用品製造商，在禮拜四休市後宣布，由於對美國的零售環境還是存有疑慮，因此他預測盈餘和營收不會太高。

Immuno (股票代號：BLDD，上漲了 1.53 點，來到 50.10 點)
輸血儀器製造商報告第二季有獲利，並宣布有一千八百萬美元的淨利，相當於每股45美分的盈餘。

Shirley & Roger (股票代號：CHBS，上漲了 3.38 點來到 36.23 點)
女性服裝零售商宣布第四季的盈餘有 29% 的成長，主要是因為新商店的強勁銷售，但該公司仍警告，已經展店一年的點，銷售可能會比之前預期的 7% 還要低。

請注意有些動詞後面會接 n.p.，有些則接 n. clause，這些細節你在語庫 8.5 中應該就已經都學會了。

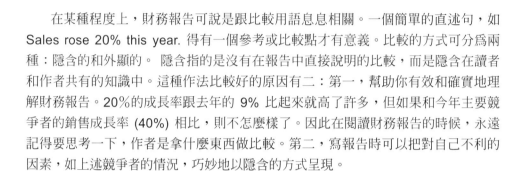

比較用語

在某種程度上，財務報告可說是跟比較用語息息相關。一個簡單的直述句，如 Sales rose 20% this year. 得有一個參考或比較點才有意義。比較的方式可分為兩種：隱含的和外顯的。 隱含指的是沒有在報告中直接說明的比較，而是隱含在讀者和作者共有的知識中。這種作法比較好的原因有二：第一，幫助你有效和確實地理解財務報告。20%的成長率跟去年的 9% 比起來就高了許多，但如果和今年主要競爭者的銷售成長率 (40%) 相比，則不怎麼樣了。因此在閱讀財務報告的時候，永遠記得要思考一下，作者是拿什麼東西做比較。第二，寫報告時可以把對自己不利的因素，如上述競爭者的情況，巧妙地以隱含的方式呈現。

而外顯則是指在報告中直接明示的比較，大部分的比較也屬於此類，請做以下 Task，幫助你理解比較用語。

TASK 8.14
請閱讀下面的報告和表格，找出比較用語。

【背景說明】
　　Rhonson & Thomson 是一家全球性的快速消費品 (FMCG) 公司，專賣美容保健商品，如洗髮精、香水、止汗劑和保養品。Rhonson & Thomson 在台灣的業務經理於三月份時寫了這份報告，比較兩個主要產品線——女性和男性美容用品——在去年和前年的銷售成績。

> 　　Overall, sales of all main brands have been down this year compared with last year. This is probably due to the fact that consumer spending in general was down owing to fears about cross-straight relations. The best performer last year was *Whiteface*, with sales of 20,000 units, down by 3,000 units from the year before. Other brands

W o r d   L i s t

FMCG (fast-moving consumer goods) 快速消費品

in the female sector also did worse than expected, with *Venus* down 9%, *Outer Beauty* down 7% and *Freedom Hair* down 3%. All products in this sector did worse than targeted.

　　In the men's segment, sales were higher than previously forecast, and topped analysts' estimates for this segment, creating hopes that this segment will see strong growth in the future. This good performance is mainly thanks to the efforts of the ad agency, who did a fabulous job. Sales of *You Butch Thing* were up 20%, *Wild Tiger* up 15.4% and *Mechanic* up 28.9 %, doing better than any of the female products.

Female				
	Whiteface	*Venus*	*Outer Beauty*	*Freedom Hair*
Sales year before	23,000	17,000	45,000	58,000
Sales last year	20,000	15,470	41,850	56,260
Target	25,000	20,000	50,000	70,000
Male				
	You Butch Thing	*Wild Tiger*	*Mechanic*	
Sales year before	12,000	19,000	16,000	
Sales last year	14,400	21,926	20,624	
Target	14,000	20,000	20,000	

答案 ▶

請研讀下面的語庫，確實瞭解比較用語。

報告 必備語庫 8.6 ▮▶

• … against …	• … the lowest …
• … compared with …	• … the most …
• … over budget.	• … the worst …
• … over target.	• … the best …
• … than analysts' expectations.	• … up from a year earlier.
• … than expected.	• … down from a year earlier.
• … than forecast.	• … matched analysts' estimates.
• … than predicted.	• … topped analysts' forecasts.
• … than previously forecast.	• … was/were better (than X) …
• … than previously reported.	• … was/were higher (than X) …
• … than previously stated.	• … was/were less (than X) …
• … than targeted.	• … was/were lower (than X) …
• … was/were up …	• … was/were more (than X) …
• … was/were down …	• … was/were worse (than X) …
• … was/were the same (as X) …	• … (did) better (than X) …
• … up …	• … (did) less (than X) …
• … down …	• … (did) more (than X) …
• … the highest …	• … (did) worse (than X) …
• … the least …	

★ 📂 語庫小叮嚀

◆ 通常只有在比較不同的貨幣匯率時會用 … against … 。請看例句。

The yen rose against the dollar.

◆ 請注意哪些 MWIs 是 chunks，哪些是 set-phrases。另外須注意的是這些 set-phrases 大部分都出現在句子的最後。

◆ Did 或其他任何動詞都可以和比較的 chunks，如 better than、less than 等一起使用。請看例句。

1. Sales last year did better than the year before.

2. Sales last year performed better than the year before.

3. This product sold better last year than the year before.

TASK 8.15

請再回頭閱讀一次 Task 8.14 的報告，找出語庫中的比較用語，在下面畫底線並注意用法。

TASK 8.16

利用 Task 8.14 的表格，造出六個句子，比較其中的資訊。

答案 ▶

以下是我的參考例句，你寫的答案可能和我的截然不同，但希望你在仔細學習這些例句後，對使用此類用語會更有自信。

1. *Whiteface* performed better than *Venus* last year.
2. *You Butch Thing* topped analysts' estimates.
3. *Venus* did not match analysts' estimates last year.
4. *Wild Tiger* was 1,926 units over target.
5. *Mechanic* did better than targeted.
6. Sales of *Freedom Hair* were down from a year earlier.

原因和結果的用語

　　財務報告的最後一個元素，就是描述數字出現變化的原因或預測變化結果的用語。最後這個元素不容易用，因為數字變化的背後有太多原因，並非每次都能有把握地知道銷售量、成本、市場佔有率或股價為什麼會改變，而且有時你也必須解釋數字變化的原因，或數字變化的預測結果。在本章的最後一個章節裡，便是要教你這方面的用語。

TASK 8.17

請再次閱讀 Task 8.14 的報告，並將原因或結果用語畫底線。

TASK 8.18

請將下面的 MWIs 分類，填入表格中。

1. ... after + n. clause
2. ... after n.p. ...
3. ... as + n. clause
4. ... because of n.p. ...
5. ... because of the fact that + n. clause
6. ... because + n. clause
7. ... due to n.p. ...
8. ... despite n.p. ...
9. ... due to the fact that + n. clause
10. ... following n.p. ...
11. ... owing to n.p. ...
12. ... owing to the fact that + n. clause
13. ... thanks to n.p. ...
14. ... thanks to the fact that + n. clause
15. ... Ving ...

Reason	Result

答案

請研讀下面的語庫,並閱讀語庫小叮嚀。

報告 必備語庫 **8.7** ▶︎   (原因和結果的 chunks)

Reason (原因)	Result (結果)
• … thanks to n.p. … • … thanks to the fact that + n. clause • … owing to n.p. … • … owing to the fact that + n. clause • … after n.p. … • … after + n. clause • … following n.p. … • … as + n. clause • … due to n.p. … • … due to the fact that + n. clause • … because of n.p. … • … because of the fact that + n. clause • … because + n. clause • … despite + n.p. …	• … Ving …

★ 🗂 語庫小叮嚀

◆ 注意到了嗎?描寫原因的用語遠比描寫結果的用語來的多。這是因為解釋原因比猜測結果容易,原因是回顧過去的;結果卻是預測未來,預測未來從不是件簡單的事情,對吧?

◆ 使用原因 chunks 時,請注意後面是該接 n.p. 或 n. clause。

TASK 8.19

請使用適當的原因或結果用語,將下面表格中的兩欄結合起來。不要忘了在必要時改變第二欄裡的動詞。請見範例。

1.	revenue for the quarter rose 6%	match analysts' estimates
2.	the share price of Nortel Networks rose	the announcement of a Q4 loss of 16%
3.	chip shares bounced back	the Bank of America says the sector would probably trend upwards
4.	the Toronto SE 300 closed up 0.98%	post a slim 0.17% gain on the week
5.	sales were higher in January and February	consumer confidence rise in December
6.	costs were down to NT$20 million	yield margins of 4.40%
7.	consumer confidence rose in December	strengthen the argument that there is a recovery on its way
8.	the head office has raised its Q2 projections for our region	strong demand for personal computers
9.	research in Movement shares rose sharply	snap back after three days of selling
10.	the price of crude oil jumped	OPEC members agree to cut production
11.	the price of business insurance soared	more than $300 million in claims from Sep.11

例句 ▶

1. Revenue for the quarter rose 6%, matching analysts' estimates.

答案 ▶

以下提供我的參考答案。

2. The share price of Nortel Networks rose despite the announcement of a Q4 loss of 16%.

W o r d　　L i s t

projection [ˌprəˈdʒɛkʃən] *n.* 預測；推測
yield [jild] *v.* 帶來（收益等）

claim [klæm] *n.*（對保險公司的）索賠

3. Chip shares bounced back after the Bank of America said the sector would probably trend upwards.

4. The Toronto SE 300 closed up 0.98%, posting a slim 0.17% gain on the week.

5. Sales were higher in January and February as consumer confidence rose in December.

6. Costs were down to NT$20 million, yielding margins of 4.40%.

7. Consumer confidence rose in December, strengthening the argument that there is a recovery on its way.

8. The head office has raised its Q2 projections for our region because of strong demand for personal computers.

9. Research in Movement shares rose sharply, snapping back after three days of selling.

10. The price of crude oil jumped, thanks to the fact that OPEC members agreed to cut production.

11. The price of business insurance soared because of more than $300 million in claims from Sept. 11.

　　我想你用的 chunks 一定不大一樣，但希望你有用心注意你的 n.p. 和 n. clause 都用對了。

　　好，本章的學習即將結束，但在這之前，請再回頭閱讀一次 Task 8.1 中的報告。

TASK 8.20

請再次閱讀 Task 8.1，將本章中所教的財務報告六大元素 MWIs 畫底線。你覺得自己對這六大元素的理解進步了多少呢？

答案▶

請以本章裡的七大語庫來核對答案。希望你現在比剛開始學習本章時更能掌握這六大元素。本章很長而且有些地方不容易，若你覺得用文字描述數字很難，建議你慢慢來，按部就班學。先從描述數字變化開始，然後納入對數據和時間的敘述，並練習用引述用語，最後再思考如何運用對自己有利的比較用語，以及衡量是否有必要解釋原因或預測結果等。一個元素接一個元素學，一句一句來。或許剛開始的學習速度不

快，但勤能補拙，我保證！

你也可以閱讀其他財務報告（當然必須是由英文人士寫的），練習找出其中的六大元素。

在本章結束之前，請回到引言的學習清單，確定每個項目都吸收了。

Part **3**
語感甦活區

Word Partnerships
語庫表

引言與學習目標

第三部分的語庫分為幾個主題,每個主題會專門含括一個特定的商業功能或部門,並列出 word partnerships 語庫表,此外,更收錄了一些關鍵字例句。若你是在這些部門服務,你在寫作提案或報告時,這些 word partnerships 語庫表就會派上用場。這些語庫的功能分類如下:

語庫分類	
銷售	p. 198
生產製造	p. 203
行銷	p. 207
財務	p. 212
人員	p. 216
管理	p. 219

如何使用 word partnerships 語庫表:

• 我接下來要給你個小指導,教你如何使用這個語庫表。
• 一旦你瞭解使用方式後,只要選擇你目前服務的部門,並花點時間研讀這些符合你需求的語庫表就可以了。遇到不熟悉的語彙時,我建議你查閱英英字典,而且最好是商英字典。
• 本書末收錄有所有 word partnerships 的索引,裡面有提案或報告範例曾出現過的語彙,方便你用來查詢這些語彙,並再次注意他們在文章中的使用方式。

提案與報告 必備語庫 1

研讀下列 word partnerships 語庫表以及例句。

v.	adj.	n.
• accept • back	• concrete • controversial	**proposal (concerning sth.)** **proposal (for sth.)**

• block	• excellent	
• come up with	• financial	
• consider	• marketing	
• discuss	• detailed	
• make		**proposal (concerning sth.)**
• oppose		**proposal (for sth.)**
• outline		
• put forward		
• reject		
• submit		
• support		
• write		

例句 ▶

- *The regional office decided not to back this proposal. Several regional directors blocked it.*
- *Someone on the sales team wrote an excellent proposal for increasing sales.*
- *I put forward a detailed proposal concerning this issue at the last board meeting.*
- *Unfortunately, my proposal was rejected by the board.*
- *We need to come up with a set of concrete proposals for how to deal with this.*

★ 🗂 語庫小叮嚀

- ◆ Word partnerships 語庫表裡有三欄：一、重點單字（以粗體表示），通常是名詞；二、最常跟這個重點單字一起使用的動詞；三、最常跟這個名詞一起使用的形容詞或名詞。
- ◆ 語庫表的閱讀方式應由左到右，選擇最能表達你意思的動詞或形容詞配對在一起。語庫表下方的例句可讓你更明瞭這些 MWIs 在句中的使用方式。
- ◆ 你可以同時使用多個形容詞，或者一個都不用。

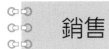 銷售

好了，練習一次後，我想你應該有能力自行研讀接下來的語庫表。

提案與報告 必備語庫 2 ▶

v.	adj.		n.
• attract	• big	• long-standing	
• be	• commercial	• loyal	
• deal with	• dissatisfied	• major	
• get	• domestic	• new	
• have	• favored	• overseas	**customer**
• serve	• good	• potential	
	• important	• private	
	• happy	• prospective	
	• international	• satisfied	
	• key	• unhappy	
	• large		

例句 ▶

- *We need to attract new domestic customers.*
- *They are one of our long-standing customers.*
- *I worked really hard to get this key customer.*
- *We need better procedures for dealing with dissatisfied customers.*
- *I serve all overseas customers.*

 W o r d   L i s t

prospective [prə`spɛktɪv] *adj.* 有希望的；預期的

提案與報告 必備語庫 3 ▐▶

n.	n.	
customer	• account • base • care • complaint • demand • inquiry • needs • order	• profile • record • relations • satisfaction • service • support • survey

例句 ▶

• *There has been a big customer demand for this type of service.*
• *We need to train all staff in the new customer service procedures.*
• *We need to offer better post-sale customer support.*
• *We should try to expand our customer base with a new range of products.*
• *Good customer relations are the secret of success in this industry.*

提案與報告 必備語庫 4 ▐▶

v.	adj.	n.
• cancel • fulfill • have • meet • place • put in • receive • win • fill • ship	• advance • bulk • large • outstanding • small	**order (for sth.)**

例句 ▶

- *They have just put in an order for 200 units.*
- *They have just placed a bulk order.*
- *In order for us to fulfill this order, we will need to ask for a 10% deposit in advance.*
- *I don't think we can meet this order on time.*
- *They called earlier asking about their outstanding order.*
- *We'll ship your order in 24 hours.*

提案與報告 必備語庫 5 ▶

v.	adj.		n.
• account for	• annual	• direct	
• achieve	• domestic	• international	
• have	• export	• net	
• generate	• foreign	• overseas	
• boost	• global	• poor	**sales**
	• good	• quarterly	
	• gross	• strong	
	• healthy	• total	
	• high	• worldwide	
	• huge	• modest	

例句 ▶

- *Europe accounts for 38% of all sales.*
- *This year we have achieved record gross sales.*
- *We need to try to generate better overseas sales.*
- *This year we have had poor export sales.*
- *This campaign boosted worldwide sales.*

boost [bust] *v.* 推動   gross [gros] *adj.* 總體的；粗略的

提案與報告 必備語庫 6

n.	n.		v.
sales	• department	• report	• decline
	• figures	• result	• drop
	• force	• revenue	• exceed
	• growth	• slump	• fall
	• level	• staff	• go down
	• performance	• target	• go up
	• personnel	• tax	• grow
	• presentation	• team	• improve
	• promotion	• value	• increase
	• rep	• volume	• reach
			• rise
			• rocket
			• slump
			• soar

例句

- *I'm working on the annual sales report at the moment.*
- *Our quarterly sales results are up from the previous quarter.*
- *The sales promotion has boosted sales by 4%.*
- *Our sales team is excellent.*
- *The new sales rep has done a great job.*

W o r d   L i s t

rep [rɛp] *n.* 推銷人；代表
slump [slʌmp] *n./v.* 暴跌；不景氣

rocket [ˈrɑkɪt] *v.* 迅速上升；猛漲
soar [sor] *v.* 猛增；暴漲

提案與報告 必備語庫 7 ▶

v.	n.	adj.	n.
• buy	• commercial	• good	
• develop	• consumer	• household	
• launch	• end	• industrial	
• market	• final	• innovative	
• produce		• high quality	**product**
• promote		• right	
• sell			
• withdraw			

例句 ▶

- *We sell a wide range of products.*
- *We produce innovative, high quality products.*
- *The end product looks really great.*
- *The finished product will be on sale at the end of the year.*
- *We are currently developing a new industrial product.*

W o r d   L i s t

launch [lɔntʃ] *v.* 推出；猛力展開
withdraw [wɪðˋdrɔ] *v.* 離開；退出

innovative [ˋɪnoͺvetɪv] *adj.* 創新的

生產製造

提案與報告 必備語庫 8 ▶

v.		adj.	n.
• be in	• increase	• annual	
• begin	• speed up	• efficient	
• boost	• start	• full	
• cut back on	• step up	• level of	**production**
• go into	• stop	• mass	
• go out of	• suspend	• small scale	
• halt			

例句 ▶

• *Due to increased demand, we have stepped up production on this line.*
• *We had a problem with quality control, so we had to suspend production for two weeks.*
• *We began production of this model two years ago.*
• *We're moving towards mass production of this model.*
• *Thanks to your proposals, we are seeing very efficient production.*

提案與報告 必備語庫 9 ▶

n.	n.		v.
	• capacity	• plant	• increase
	• costs	• process	• rise
production	• level	• team	• fall
	• line	• volumew	
	• methods		

W o r d L i s t

halt [hɔlt] *v.* 停止；終止

例句 ▶

• *Production costs are rising all the time.*
• *We need to try to boost production volume to meet all our orders.*
• *Our production team is one of the best in the business.*
• *The new production plant in China is almost completed.*
• *We need to search for new production methods which will help us to reduce costs.*

提案與報告 必備語庫 10 ▶

v.	adj.	n.	n.
• bring down • calculate • cover • cut • estimate • incur • keep down • lower • meet • pay • recoup • reduce	• administrative • considerable • enormous • escalating • fuel • great • high • huge • low • potential • rising • running • variable	• labor • materials • production • R&D (research and development) • transport • travel • wage • fixed • inventory	**costs**

例句 ▶

• *We need to try to reduce our variable costs.*
• *If we could recoup our R&D costs on this product, I would be happy.*

recoup [rɪ`kup] *v.* 回收（成本）　　　　escalating [`ɛskə͵letɪŋ] *adj.* 逐步高升的
administrative [əd`mɪnə͵stretɪv] *adj.* 管理的；行政的

- *We are going to incur rising fuel and transport costs because of the price of oil.*
- *I estimate our potential costs to be huge.*
- *Our running costs last quarter were too high. We need to lower them.*

提案與報告 必備語庫 11 ▶

v.	adj.	n.
• carry • dispose of • have • hold • keep • reduce • replace	• adequate • existing • high • large • reserve	**stocks (of sth.)**

例句 ▶

- *I'm keeping large reserve stocks of our most popular products.*
- *We need to try to dispose of our existing stocks of this product in order to reduce inventory costs.*
- *Please make sure to hold a buffer stock of our main raw materials in case supplies run low.*
- *We already have high stocks of raw cotton.*
- *Do we carry adequate stocks of our main raw materials?*

W o r d L i s t

reserve [rɪˋzɝv] *adj.* 預備的；準備的   buffer [ˋbʌfə] *n.* 緩衝物

提案與報告 必備語庫 12 ▶

v.	adj.	n.
• be • disrupt • ensure • find • get • have • maintain • obtain	• dwindling • essential • large • limited • regular • reliable • small • steady • sufficient	**supply (of sth.)**

例句 ▶

- *There is a dwindling supply of an essential raw material.*
- *We need to find a reliable supply of materials.*
- *In the current crisis, we must maintain a steady supply of materials and equipment.*
- *I must warn you that we only have a limited supply of our main raw materials left.*
- *Supplies of certain materials have been disrupted due to the war.*

dwindling [ˋdwɪndḷɪŋ] *adj.* 逐漸減少的；逐漸變小的

行銷

提案與報告 必備語庫 **13**

v.	adj.	n.	n.
• come up with	• aggressive		• agency
• develop	• direct		• campaign
• do	• effective		• department
• implement	• global	**product**	• exercise
• improve	• good		• strategy
• plan	• local		• tool
• recommend	• new		
	• poor		

例句

- *Our marketing department has come up with an aggressive global market-ing strategy.*
- *We need to implement a local marketing campaign to try to boost sales.*
- *The marketing agency we are using at the moment is recommending a direct marketing campaign.*
- *The cool card is a useful marketing tool.*
- *We're developing a local marketing strategy.*

Word List

aggressive [əˈgrɛsɪv] *adj.* 有進取精神的

提案與報告 必備語庫 14

v.	adj.	n.
• be	• competitive	
• break into	• global	
• capture	• home	
• come on to	• international	
• corner	• mass	
• create	• overseas	**market**
• develop	• steady	
• flood	• strong	
• get into	• thriving	
• penetrate	• weak	
• put sth. on to		
• supply		

例句

- *This market is very competitive.*
- *Several new products similar to our own have recently come onto the market.*
- *The market is being flooded by cheaper goods from overseas.*
- *As part of our growth strategy, I recommend penetrating the Chinese market.*
- *We have successfully cornered the domestic market for this type of product.*

 W o r d   L i s t

corner [ˋkɔrnɚ] *v.* 壟斷（市場）；囤積（貨品）
penetrate [ˋpɛnəˏtret] *v.* 洞察；看透

thriving [ˋθraɪvɪŋ] *adj.* 興旺；茁壯成長

提案與報告 必備語庫 15 ▶

n.	n.	
market	• conditions • leader • position • price • research	• sector • segment • share • trend • value

例句 ▶

• *Market conditions are favorable for this type of product.*
• *Our market share is growing steadily.*
• *We aim to become the market leader in three years.*
• *We must try to steal some market share from our competitors.*
• *This market sector is already very crowded.*

提案與報告 必備語庫 16 ▶

adj.	adj.	n.
• competitive • constructive • direct mail • informative • mass • persuasive • point-of-sale	**advertising**	• agency • budget • campaign • strategy

例句 ▶

• *A direct mail advertising campaign would be the most effective in this case.*
• *Because the product is quite complex, we need to have an informative advertising strategy.*

• *Mass advertising in all media is too expensive for us at the moment.*
• *I think we should try more point-of-sale advertising. It's cheap and effective.*

提案與報告 必備語庫 **17** ▶

v.		adj.		n.
• accept	• make prepare	• annual	• in-depth	
• appear in	• present	• audit	• initial	
• compile	• produce	• confidential	• interim	
• consider	• read	• critical	• joint	
• deliver	• release	• detailed	• market	
• discuss	• submit	• draft	• misleading	**report**
• draw up	• type up	• due diligence	• preliminary	**(on sth.)**
• give sb.	• write	• encouraging	• progress	
• issue		• false	• quarterly	
		• final	• research	
		• financial		

例句 ▶

• *Their people in my department are compiling a joint report on this at the moment.*
• *I am in the process of drawing up a detailed report.*
• *I hope I can submit my quarterly report on Monday.*
• *The annual report was so encouraging that we decided to release it to the shareholders early.*
• *It seems that the CEO issued a misleading financial report.*

audit [ˋɔdɪt] n. 審核；查帳   compile [kəmˋpaɪl] v. 匯編；編輯
diligence [ˋdɪlədʒəns] n. 勤勉；勤奮

提案與報告 必備語庫 **18**

n.	v.	
report	• argue n.p. • argue that + n. clause • be based on n.p. • cover n.p. • demonstrate n.p. • demonstrate that + n. clause • draw attention to n.p. • draw attention to the fact that 　+ n. clause	• emphasize n.p. • emphasize that + n. clause • examine n.p. • find n.p. • find that + n. clause • list n.p. • outline n.p. • state n.p. • state that + n. clause

例句 ▶

- *This report was based on figures given to me by the accounting department.*
- *The report covers all aspects of the production process.*
- *The report draws attention to the fact that budgets have been inflated.*
- *My report outlines several problems in the marketing department.*
- *The report emphasizes that too much money is being wasted on ineffective marketing.*

demonstrate [ˋdɛmənˌstret] v. 顯示；表露　　　inflate [ɪnˋflet] v. 擴張；增加

財務

提案與報告 必備語庫 19 ▶

v.	adj.	n.	n.
• approve	• advertising		• expenditure
• be over	• annual		• deficit
• be under	• fixed		• surplus
• cut	• large		
• draw up	• limited		
• exceed	• low		
• get	• marketing		
• go over	• monthly	**budget**	
• have	• quarterly		
• keep within	• PR (public relations)		
• plan	• R&D		
• reduce	• shoestring		
• set	• tight		
• stick to	• training		
• submit	• weekly		

例句 ▶

- *We have gone over budget this quarter. This means that we need to increase our budget next quarter.*
- *Please make sure all departments keep within budget.*
- *We are prepared to approve a large advertising budget for the project.*

shoestring [ˈʃuˌstrɪŋ] *adj.* 極少的；不足的   surplus [ˈsɝpləs] *n.* 盈餘；順差
deficit [ˈdɛfɪsɪt] *n.* 不足額；赤字

- *We are in the process of drawing up an annual marketing budget for next year.*
- *Please try to cut the budget deficit in your department.*

提案與報告 必備語庫 20

v.	adj.		n.
• bring in	• after-tax	• modest	
• earn	• clear	• net	
• generate	• corporate	• operating	
• make	• excess	• pre-tax	
• realize	• first-quarter	• record	
• yield	• full-year	• short-term	**profits**
• boost	• gross	• small	
• maximize	• group	• substantial	
• increase	• half-year	• taxable	
	• handsome	• trading	
	• interim		
	• large		
	• lost		

例句

- *This product has brought in handsome pre-tax profits.*
- *We have been able to maximize short-term profits.*
- *First quarter after-tax trading profits have been excellent.*
- *The Southern region yielded record profits of NT$15 million last year.*
- *We need to find a way to generate larger interim profits.*

W o r d   L i s t

handsome [ˈhænsəm] *adj.* (金錢)可觀的

interim [ˈɪntərɪm] *adj.* 過渡期的；暫時的

213

提案與報告 必備語庫 21 ▋▶

v.		adj.		n.
• cut	• offset	• heavy	• net	
• incur	• recoup	• huge	• pre-tax	**losses**
• make	• recover	• massive	• overall	
• minimize	• suffer	• slight		

例句 ▶

- *We have incurred large losses in several regions this year.*
- *We can offset the losses we suffered last year with the profits we generated in the first quarter of this year.*
- *We need to recoup some of the heavy losses from Q2.*
- *We have suffered massive losses due to the technical problems with the product.*
- *Please try to minimize all loss.*

W o r d   L i s t

offset [ˈɔf͵sɛt] *v.* 補償；抵銷

提案與報告 必備語庫 22 ▶

adj.	n.	v.
• advanced		• collapse
• booming		• contract
• developed		• develop
• false		• expand
• flagging		• grow
• global	**economy**	• pick up
• healthy		• recover
• local		• slow
• modern		• stabilize
• regional		
• stable		
• strong		
• weak		

例句 ▶

- *Buying inferior materials just because they are cheap is a false economy, as we will incur quality control costs.*
- *The local economy is contracting, which makes it difficult to impose price increases.*
- *The economy here is extremely stable, which makes it a good place to launch financial products.*
- *The high price of oil means the regional economy will start to slow.*
- *We expect the flagging economy to recover within the next three years.*

W o r d L i s t

flagging [ˋflægɪŋ] *adj.* 衰弱的　　　　contract [ˋkɑntrækt] *v.* 使收縮；使縮小

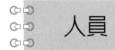 人員

提案與報告 必備語庫 **23**

v.	adj.	n.	n.
• appoint	• experienced		• development
• dismiss	• full-time		• levels
• employ	• junior		• member
• fire	• part-time		• morale
• have	• permanent	**(member of)**	• resources
• hire	• qualified	**staff**	• shortage
• lay off	• senior		• turnover
• make redundant	• skilled		
• recruit	• support		
• sack	• temporary		
• take on	• unskilled		
• train			

例句 ▶

• *We need to appoint three new full-time members of staff.*
• *If we go ahead with this merger, we'll need to lay off 200 staff.*
• *We might need to hire some temporary support staff for the duration of the project.*
• *It's very difficult to find qualified senior staff these days.*
• *The staff shortage is causing very low staff morale, which in turn contributes to high staff turnover.*

 W o r d   L i s t

redundant [rɪˋdʌndənt] *adj.* 多餘的；過剩的　　　sack [sæk] *v.* （口語）開除；解雇

提案與報告 必備語庫 24

v.	adj.	n.
• assess • deliver • enhance • improve • inhibit • measure	• all-round • business • disappointing • economic • financial • impressive • overall • sales • satisfactory	**performance**

例句

- *You need to improve your disappointing performance.*
- *We believe an incentive system will enhance sales performance.*
- *Poor morale has inhibited performance this year.*
- *We are looking for quantitative ways to assess performance.*
- *Most departments delivered an impressive performance last year.*

提案與報告 必備語庫 25

v.	n.	n.
• conduct • have • set • use	**performance**	• appraisal • evaluation • indicator • level • management • measure • standard • target

assess [əˈsɛs] *v.* 評價；對……進行評估
inhibit [ɪnˈhɪbɪt] *v.* 禁止；抑制

incentive [ɪnˈsɛntɪv] *adj.* 獎勵的；鼓勵的
quantitative [ˈkwɑntəˌtetɪv] *v.* 量化的

例句 ▶

- *We are conducting annual performance appraisals this week.*
- *I think we set performance targets too high last year.*
- *We are using a new performance management system.*
- *Performance levels are still too low.*
- *The performance indicators we have been using are not very accurate.*

提案與報告 必備語庫 26 ▶

v.	adj.	n.	n.
• do	• adequate		• course
• get	• basic		• initiative
• have	• extensive		• material
• implement	• hands-on		• needs
• offer	• initial	training	• objectives
• provide	• job-related		• opportunities
• receive	• ongoing		• package
• review	• proper		• policy
• undergo	• thorough		• program
			• provider
			• workshop

例句 ▶

- *We need to offer a basic training course to all new employees.*
- *I recommend that we review our job-related training policy.*
- *We have found an excellent training provider offering specialist training.*
- *All members of the department have undergone extensive training.*
- *An ongoing training package is one way to retain key employees.*

accurate ['ækjərɪt] *adj.* 精準的；準確的
initiative [ɪ'nɪʃətɪv] *n.* 進取心；創始力

objective [əb'dʒɛktɪv] *n.* 目標；標的
retain [rɪ'ten] *v.* 保有；維持

 管理

提案與報告 必備語庫 **27** ▮▶

v.	adj.	n.
• back • carry out • implement • launch • plan • run • set up • support	• joint • large • major • marketing • new • research	**project**

例句 ▶

- *Head Office has decided to back this project.*
- *We are in the process of carrying out a new product development project.*
- *We should set up a new marketing project.*
- *Implementing this joint project is going to be difficult.*
- *The research project was launched last year.*

提案與報告 必備語庫 **28** ▮▶

v.	adj.	n.
• achieve • analyze • come up with • get • give • have • produce • show	• better-than-expected • disappointing • good • impressive • poor • positive • surprising • worse-than-expected	**results**

例句

- *The focus group produced better-than-expected results.*
- *We did some market research and came up with some surprising results.*
- *Your sales team has produced impressive sales results this quarter.*
- *Results of the quality control tests have all been positive.*
- *We need to give the client good results.*

提案與報告 必備語庫 29

v.		adj.		n.
• analyze	• grasp	• awkward	• political	
• assess	• have	• complex	• risky	
• avoid	• improve	• critical	• serious	
• be	• lead to	• current	• simple	
• be faced with	• respond	• delicate	• stable	
• be placed in	• result in	• difficult	• strategic	
• bring about	• review	• economic	• stressful	
• create	• take advan-	• embarrassing	• tricky	**situation**
• defuse	tage of	• financial	• unstable	
• discuss	• take control of	• general	• whole	
• examine	• understand	• international	• win-win	
• face	• weigh up	• legal		
• get into		• local		
		• no-win		
		• overall		

例句

- *We are faced with a tricky political situation here.*
- *I don't think the CEO has grasped the complex nature of the situation in this market.*
- *We are trying to defuse this embarrassing situation, but it may take time.*

 W o r d   L i s t

defuse [dɪˋfjuz] v. 緩和不安；解決衝突或窘境

220

• *I am weighing up the economic situation, and will give you a more detailed response in a few days.*
• *Our competitors' actions have placed us in a no-win situation, and I recommend withdrawal from the market.*

提案與報告 必備語庫 **30**

v.	adj.		n.
• be	• additional	• key	
• consider	• common	• main	
• depend on	• contributing	• political	
• take into account	• critical	• social	**factor**
	• economic	• special	
	• environmental	• the single most impor-	
	• external	tant	
	• internal	• vital	

例句

• *There are many external factors which are affecting our performance this year.*
• *We should take into account the special environmental factors associated with this project.*
• *Customers consider a number of factors when deciding what product to purchase.*
• *Success in this market depends on many factors, the vital factor being price.*
• *While the company image is a contributing factor, I don't think it's the key factor.*

take into account 對……加以考慮
contributing [kən'trɪbjətɪŋ] *adj.* 有貢獻的；有幫助的

external [ɪk'stɜnl] *adj.* 外部的
internal [ɪn'tɜnl] *adj.* 內部的

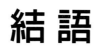

結　語

道別與總結

　　恭喜你，本書的學習到此告一段落。知道嗎？你學到的知識頗為豐富呢！我們研讀了如何撰寫成功的提案和報告，還有資料的蒐集、衡量和呈現方法。我們學到時態的正確用法，可用來有效地表達你所指的時間。我們也探討過如何寫出正式或非正式的提案，並學會描述提案執行後可能得到的結果和遇到的情況，以便確實評估提案。緊接著我們又學了如何撰寫聯繫報告、會議報告和專案進度報告，最後並研究了財務報告的六大元素。在學習的過程中你做了大量的 Task，未來不只運用這些用語的功力大增，實際寫報告和提案時更是信心百倍。除此之外，透過本書的 Leximodel 字串學習法，你對英文的瞭解和認識也更上一層樓了。

　　你也許還記得在前言中，我請你做過一個 Task，加強對 chunks、set-phrases 和 word partnerships 的認識。現在不妨再做一次這個 Task，鞏固本書所有學到的知識。

TASK 結語

請閱讀下列報告，用三種不同顏色的筆分別在 chunks、set-phrases 和 word partnerships 下畫底線，然後填入下表中。請見範例。

　　These days, while many companies in China, Taiwan, Hong Kong, Singapore, and South Korea are trying to find ways to raise capital, many of their counterparts in Thailand, Malaysia, and Indonesia are still trying hard to pay off their debt.

　　Three and a half years after the regional financial crisis, many companies in Southeast Asia are still restructuring their businesses to strengthen their balance sheets. A majority have sold or shut their non-core or non-profitable units to raise funds, while others are negotiating with scores of creditors to extend their loan repayment period.

　　For a good example, look no further than Thailand's Silom City Holdings, Inc., which was once one of the country's most heavily

---

indebted companies. Now, however, Silom owes creditors just US$110 million, a far cry from the US$542 million it owed at the end of 1997. Its sales and profits last year were US$322 million and US$21 million respectively.

Described by its peers as a model for Thailand's debt restructuring effort, Silom City Holdings sold US$917 million worth of non-core assets by 2000, among them its sanitary goods, electrical products, and packaging units, to raise cash. At the same time, it also sold a 25 percent stake to the Swiss company Wunderbar in exchange for funding and management assistance to help revitalize the company.

Set-phrases	Chunks	Word Partnerships
• *For a good example, look no further than …*	• *… try to …*	• *raise capital*

答案 ▶

請以下表核對答案。希望現在你完成這個 Task 的速度已經比第一次快多了，對自己的答案也有信心，此外，不妨拿這次的答案跟上次的作比較，看看你進步了多少。

Set-phrases	Chunks	Word partnerships
• For a good example, look no further than … • At the same time, …	• … try to … • these days … • pay off … • negotiate with … • scores of … • one of the … • a far cry from … • at the end of … • a model for … • sell sth. to sb. … • in exchange for …	• raise capital • find ways to • regional financial crisis • balance sheets • raise funds • loan repayment period • debt restructuring effort • non-core assets • sanitary goods • electrical products • packaging units • raise cash • management assistance

現在你已經學會如何辨識報告中的 chunks、set-phrases 和 word partnerships，未來這個能力絕對有利於英文寫作或一般的英語學習。接下來我要教你如何繼續加強現有的英語能力！

充分利用本書

1. 多利用本書的附錄當作參考工具。
2. 每隔幾週回來翻閱一下本書，複習相關單元中的各個語庫，並閱讀語庫小叮嚀，以免忘掉 MWIs 的一些重要用法以及細節！
3. 就如同我在前言中提過的，請每週花 20 分鐘閱讀書中的範例提案與報告，在所有 chunks 下畫底線並整理成一份筆記。有的則可以寫在本書後面的目標頁中，方便以後寫報告時隨時取用。
4. 雖然整理 MWIs 費時費力，但努力絕不會白費。

保持你的英文水平

保持英語能力的方法很多，我整理出了六種，如下：

1. 每天背幾個新字串。

你可以從報紙、網路或收到的電子郵件和報告（英文為母語人士所寫的）中，挑出一些新字串。也就是 chunks、set-phrases 或 word partnerships，因為若只是光背單字，對學習英文的用處不大。

2. 選擇難度高、不熟悉或沒看過的用語。

記住，天底下沒有難的字串，只有不熟悉的字串。有些字串乍看之下很陌生，但只要多加練習，一定會越熟悉。就算起初看了覺得不認識，只要多練習幾次，不久就會吸收成為你詞彙的一部分了。等到你覺得運用自如時，就表示你已經學會這個字串，能夠繼續研讀下一個新字串了。

3. 刻意運用新字串。

多加利用本書附錄的語庫，寫提案或報告時，記得要實際運用這些你剛學到的新用語，用久了，自然而然就會記得起來，內化成為詞彙中的一部分了。

4. 如果可以，盡量避免使用已知和運用自如的字串。

大多人總是反覆使用同樣、已知、運用自如的字串，也因為如此，他們的英文永遠停留在原地，不會進步！

5. 勇於實驗和嘗試，並從錯誤中學習。

用字遣詞會出錯，是因為試圖發揮創意，實驗不同語文的用法，但這是學習語言過程中很重要的一環。從不犯錯並不表示你很優秀（除了極少數的例外），事實上可能只是因為你沒有嘗試使用新用語罷了！

6. 留意生活周遭遇到的語文。

為自己創造出一個小型的英語環境。把喜歡的英文網站加入我的最愛中，花些時間看有興趣的文章，抄下看到的 chunks 和 word partnerships。將收集到的提案或報告儲存在一個特定的資料夾中，花些時間研究裡面的 MWIs。研究一再證明，加強英文最重要的方法除了閱讀之外還是閱讀！

謝謝你跟著我一起學習和研讀本書，希望你自覺有所收穫。如果現在你對寫英文提案和報告信心百倍，我就算是成功地幫助你提升了英文寫作能力，這可是對我的一種肯定呢！

祝寫作愉快！

附錄

 附錄一：提案與報告必備語庫

提案 必備語庫 2.1 ▶ 動詞三態   p.55

become	became	become	leave	left	left
begin	began	begun	let	let	let
bring	brought	brought	make	made	made
come	came	come	meet	met	met
do	did	done	pay	paid	paid
feel	felt	felt	put	put	put
find	found	found	read	read	read
get	got	got/gotten	say	said	said
give	gave	given	see	saw	seen
go	went	gone	send	sent	sent
have	had	had	set	set	set
hear	heard	heard	take	took	taken
hold	held	held	tell	told	told
keep	kept	kept	think	thought	thought
know	knew	known	understand	understood	understood
learn	learned	learned	write	wrote	written

提案 必備語庫 2.2 ▶ 過去與現在時間的 chunks   p.56

Past Time Chunks （過去時間 chunks）	Present Time Chunks （現在時間 chunks）
• last year • last quarter • during that time • ago • yesterday • then • in 1999	• this year • during this time • year-to-date • this week • this quarter • so far

提案 必備語庫 2.3 ▶ 現在時間的動詞與時間 chunks　　　　　p.62

	常用動詞	時間 chunks
現在進行式	• wait • hope • try • work • change	• currently • still • these days
現在完成式	• change • complete • become • ask • achieve • decide • develop • finish • find • improve • happen • receive • send • speak • write	• since • for • yet • already • recently • ever • just • so far • lately • these days • never … before

提案 必備語庫 2.4 ▶ 預測字串　　　　　p.70

• … n.p. … prospects are fairly limited. • … envisage n.p. … • … be tipped to V … • … analysts predict that + n. clause … • … look set to V … • There's every/little chance of n.p. …	• It looks as though + n. clause … • There's every/little chance that + n. clause … • It looks like + n. clause … • It is highly probable that + n. clause … • The indications are that + n. clause …

• There's every/little chance of Ving …	• … be due to V …
• It is unlikely that + n. clause ...	• The outlook is adj. …
• It looks like being n.p.	• … in the short term …
• … be expected to V …	• … in the long term …
• … envisage that + n. clause. …	• … in the medium term …
• … will probably V …	• … prospects (for sth.) are looking good/bad …
	• … might V …

提案 必備語庫 3.1 ▶ 建議的 verb chunks   p.79

• … recommend that + n. clause …	• … should not V …
• … recommend n.p …	• … ought to V …
• … propose that + n. clause …	• … suggest that + n. clause …
• … propose n.p. …	• … propose to V …
• … propose Ving …	• … should V …
• … ought not to V …	• … recommend Ving …
• … suggest n.p. …	• … suggest Ving …

提案 必備語庫 3.2 ▶ 建議的 set-phrases   p.86

• I would like to make the following proposal(s).	• My recommendation here is for n.p. …
• It is recommended that + n. clause …	• It is suggested that + n. clause …
• My suggestion here is to V …	• My suggestion here is that + n. clause…
• I would like to make the following recommendation(s).	• I would like to make the following suggestion(s).
• My recommendation here is that + n. clause …	• My proposal here is that + n. clause …
• It is proposed that + n. clause …	• My recommendation here is to V …
• My proposal here is to V …	• My suggestion here is for n.p. …
• My proposal here is for n.p. …	

提案 必備語庫 4.1 ▶ 描述目的和預期結果的字串　　　　p.99

Result（結果）	Purpose（目的）
• This will result in n.p. … • This will V … • From our experience, … • These strategies/recommendations will ensure that + n. clause … • This strategy/recommendation will facilitate sth. in Ving • … lead to n.p. … • … result in n.p. … • … in such a way as to V … • … in such a way that + n. clause … • … otherwise + n. clause …	• … in order that + n. clause … • … in order to V … • … so as to V … • … so that + n. clause … • … to V …

提案 必備語庫 4.2 ▶ 描述假設情況及其結果的字串　　　　p.104

Conditions（假設語氣）	Consequences （結果）
• If we do that, … • If we V, … • If we don't V …, • Unless we V …, • Should we V …,	• … will V … • … may V … • … might V … • … could V … • … will probably V … • it will have the effect of Ving … • … may end up Ving … • it's likely that + n. clause … • … be likely to V … • there's every chance that + n. clause … • there's a strong possibility of n.p/Ving … • there is every/no/little likelihood of n.p./Ving …

- there's every chance of n.p. …
- it's possible that + n. clause …
- it's unlikely that + n. clause …
- there's a strong possibility that + n. clause …
- … be unlikely to V …
- there is every/no/little likelihood that + n. clause …

 提案 必備語庫 **4.3** ▶ 對比字串   p.108

• However, … • On the other hand, … • Still, …	• On the contrary, … • By contrast, … • Then again, …

報告 必備語庫 **6.1** ▶ 描述已完成／未完成事項的用語   p.133

Describing Completed Results （描述已完成的結果）	Describing Uncompleted Activities （描述未完成的活動）
• We've p.p. … • We've just p.p. … • We've already p.p. … • We've managed to V … • We've decided to V … • We've been able to V … • … so that's done. • … so that's ready to go. • … has now been finalized. • … has now been completed.	• We've been Ving … • We're trying to V … • We're in the process of Ving … • We are working round the clock on this. • We haven't p.p. yet … • We haven't managed to V yet. • We're having problems with n.p. … • We're having problems Ving … • Right now we're in the middle of Ving … • … so that's not ready yet. • … so that still needs more work. • … so that still needs to be done. • … we have been a bit delayed.

報告 必備語庫 6.2 ▮▶ 描述未來的計畫或安排   p.136

Describing Arrangements（描述安排的事項）
• We're going to V ...
• We're Ving ...
• We're taking steps to V ...
• We intend to V ...
• We're making arrangements for n.p. ...
• We're making arrangements to V ...
• We've made arrangements for n.p. ...
• We've made arrangements to V ...
• Our intention is to V ...
• Our plan is to V ...
• We hope to V ...
• We've still got to V ...
• We plan to V ...

報告 必備語庫 7.1 ▮▶ 陳述意見的 verb chunks（後面接 n. clause）   p.154

• acknowledged that + n. clause	認知到
• admitted that + n. clause	承認了
• agreed that + n. clause	同意了
• announced that + n. clause	宣布了
• answered that + n. clause	答覆了
• argued that + n. clause	主張要
• assured sb. that + n. clause	向某人保証要……
• claimed that + n. clause	主張要
• commented that + n. clause	評論說
• confirmed that + n. clause	證實了
• denied that + n. clause	否定了
• estimated that + n. clause	估計了
• explained that + n. clause	解釋說
• informed sb. that + n. clause	告知說

• insisted that + n. clause	堅持要
• maintained that + n. clause	主張要
• mentioned that + n. clause	提到了
• promised that + n. clause	保証說
• recommended that + n. clause	建議要
• replied that + n. clause	回覆了
• reported that + n. clause	報告說
• requested that + n. clause	要求說
• suggested that + n. clause	提議了
• threatened that + n. clause	威脅要
• warned that + n. clause	警告說

報告 必備語庫 **7.2** ▶ 陳述意見的 verb chunks (後面接 n.p.)　　p.157

- complained about n.p.
- agreed about n.p.
- explained (about) n.p.
- warned us about n.p.

報告 必備語庫 **7.3** ▶ 傳達問題／指示的 verb chunks　　p.159

Question Reporting Verbs (傳達問題的動詞)	Instruction Reporting Verbs (傳達指示的動詞)
• asked (sb.) wh- + n. clause • asked about n.p. • inquired (as to) wh- + n. clause • inquired about n.p.	• advised sb. to V • asked sb. to V • instructed sb. to V • invited sb. to V • warned sb. to V

報告 必備語庫 7.4 ▮▸ 簡單概述某議題的 verb chunks　　　　　p.161

• acknowledged receipt of n.p.	• raised the issue of n.p.
• expressed an interest in n.p.	• reaffirmed sb.'s position on n.p.
• outlined the plans for n.p.	• stressed the importance of n.p.
• put forward a proposal for n.p.	• voiced sb.'s concerns about n.p.
• put forward a proposal to V	
• questioned the need for n.p.	

報告 必備語庫 8.1 ▮▸ 描述數字變化的 chunks（動詞用法）　　　　p.171

Movement Up （數字上升）	Movement Down （數字下降）	Very Little Movement （數字變化不大）
• … closed up …	• … closed down …	• … held steady …
• … gained …	• … declined …	• … peaked …
• … jumped …	• … dipped …	• … stabilized …
• … rallied …	• … dropped …	• … troughed …
• … picked up …	• … fell …	• … stayed the same …
• … rose …	• … shrank …	• … remained steady …
• … soared …	• … went down …	• … fluctuated …
• … bounced back …	• … withered …	• … stagnated …
• … recovered …	• … decreased …	• … hovered around …
• … shot up …	• … plunged …	
• … went up …	• … plummeted …	
• … snapped back …		
• … increased …		
• … grew …		

報告 必備語庫 8.2 ▶ 描述數字變化的 chunks（名詞用法）　　　p.174

Movement Up（數字上升）	Movement Down（數字下降）
• … a gain (of X) in Y …	• … a dramatic downturn in Y …
• … some signs of growth in Y …	• … an all-time low in Y …
• … a recovery in Y …	• … a decrease (of X) in Y …
• … a trend upwards in Y …	• … a fall (of X) in Y …
• … an upward trend in Y …	• … a record low (of X) in Y …
• … some signs of recovery in Y …	• … a slump in Y …
• … a record high (of X) in Y …	• … a downward trend in Y …
• … an all-time high (of X) in Y …	• … a trend downwards in Y …
• … an increase (of X) in Y …	• … a loss (of X) in Y …
• … a rise (of X) in Y …	• … a trough in Y …
• … a peak in Y …	• … a steady decline in Y …

報告 必備語庫 8.3 ▶ 描述數據的 chunks　　　p.179

Distance（差距）	Point（起迄點）
• … X points/units …	• … to X …
• … X percent/% …	• … from X …
• … (by) X points/units …	• … to end at X …
• … (by) X percent/% …	• … to close at X …
• … from X to Z …	• … be at X …
• … of X % …	• … at X …
• … of X points/units …	

報告 必備語庫 **8.4** ▶ 財務報告的時間 chunks   p.181

• in the last quarter (of the year)	• in the second half (of the year)
• at the end of Q2	• this quarter
• in the first quarter (of the year)	• at the end of the year
• this year	• in Q4
• in the previous quarter	• last quarter
• last year	• in Q4 of last year
• in 1999	• in Q1 of this year
• in March	• at the beginning of the year
• in the same period	• in the later half of the year
• at the same time	• at the beginning of Q2
• in the first half (of the year)	• in the early half of the year

報告 必備語庫 **8.5** ▶ 引述的 chunks   p.183

• … said + n. clause	• … warned + n. clause
• … reiterated + n. clause	• … warned about n.p. …
• … reported + n. clause	• … attributed the increase to n.p. …
• … posted n.p. …	• … announced + n. clause
• … reiterated n.p. …	• … agreed + n. clause
• … reported n.p.…	• … announced n.p. …

報告 必備語庫 **8.6** ▶ 比較用語   p.188

• … against …	• … than predicted.
• … compared with …	• … than previously forecast.
• … over budget.	• … than previously reported.
• … over target.	• … than previously stated.
• … than analysts' expectations.	• … than targeted.
• … than expected.	• … was/were up …
• … than forecast.	• … was/were down …

• ... was/were the same (as X) ...	• ... topped analysts' forecasts.
• ... up ...	• ... was/were better (than X) ...
• ... down ...	• ... was/were higher (than X) ...
• ... the highest ...	• ... was/were less (than X) ...
• ... the least ...	• ... was/were lower (than X) ...
• ... the lowest ...	• ... was/were more (than X) ...
• ... the most ...	• ... was/were worse (than X) ...
• ... the worst ...	• ... (did) better (than X) ...
• ... the best ...	• ... (did) less (than X) ...
• ... up from a year earlier.	• ... (did) more (than X) ...
• ... down from a year earlier.	• ... (did) worse (than X) ...
• ... matched analysts' estimates.	

報告 必備語庫 **8.7** ▶ 原因和結果的 chunks   p.191

Reason (原因)	Result (結果)
• ... thanks to n.p. ...	• ... Ving ...
• ... thanks to the fact that + n. clause	
• ... owing to n.p. ...	
• ... owing to the fact that + n. clause	
• ... after n.p. ...	
• ... after + n. clause	
• ... following n.p. ...	
• ... as + n. clause	
• ... due to n.p. ...	
• ... due to the fact that + n. clause	
• ... because of n.p. ...	
• ... because of the fact that + n. clause	
• ... because + n. clause	
• ... despite + n.p. ...	

附錄二：學習目標記錄表

利用這張表來設立你的學習目標和記錄你的學習狀況，以找出改進之道。

第一欄：寫下你接下來一週預定學習或使用的字串。
第二欄：寫下你在當週實際使用該字串的次數。
第三欄：寫下你使用該字串時遇到的困難或該注意的事項。

預計使用的字串	使用次數	附註

國家圖書館出版品預行編目資料

愈忙愈要學英文提案與報告
Quentin Brand 作；金振寧譯. －－初版. －－
臺北市：貝塔，2006〔民95〕
　　面；　　公分

　ISBN 957-729-547-9（平裝附光碟片）

　1. 企管英語－讀本

805.18　　　　　　　　　　　　94018509

愈忙愈要學英文提案與報告
Biz English for Busy People—Proposals and Reports

作　　　者 / Quentin Brand
總 編 輯 / 梁欣榮
譯　　　者 / 金振寧
執行編輯 / 廖姿菱

出　　　版 / 貝塔出版有限公司
地　　　址 / 台北市 100 館前路 12 號 11 樓
電　　　話 / (02) 2314-2525
傳　　　真 / (02) 2312-3535
客服專線 / (02) 2314-3535
客服信箱 / btservice@betamedia.com.tw
郵撥帳號 / 19493777
帳戶名稱 / 貝塔出版有限公司

總 經 銷 / 時報文化出版企業股份有限公司
地　　　址 / 桃園縣龜山鄉萬壽路二段 351 號
電　　　話 / (02) 2306-6842
傳　　　真 / (02) 2306-6842

出版日期 / 2008年12月初版二刷
定　　　價 / 280元
ISBN：957-729-547-9

Biz English for Busy People —Proposals and Reports
Copyright 2006 by Quentin Brand
Published by Beta Multimedia Publishing

喚醒你的英文語感 ！

折後釘好，直接寄回即可！

廣 告 回 信
北區郵政管理局登記證
北 台 字 第14256號
免 貼 郵 票

100 台北市中正區館前路12號11樓

 貝塔語言出版 收
Beta Multimedia Publishing

寄件者住址 □ □ □

謝謝您購買本書！！

貝塔語言擁有最優良之英文學習書籍，為提供您最佳的英語學習資訊，您可填妥此表後寄回（免貼郵票）將可不定期收到本公司最新發行書訊及活動訊息！

姓名：＿＿＿＿＿＿＿＿＿＿＿＿＿　性別：口男 口女　生日：＿＿＿年＿＿＿月＿＿＿日

電話：(公)＿＿＿＿＿＿＿＿＿(宅)＿＿＿＿＿＿＿＿＿(手機)＿＿＿＿＿＿＿＿

電子信箱：＿＿＿＿＿＿＿＿＿＿＿＿＿＿＿＿＿＿＿＿＿＿＿＿

學歷：口高中職含以下 口專科 口大學 口研究所含以上

職業：口金融 口服務 口傳播 口製造 口資訊 口軍公教 口出版

　　　口自由 口教育 口學生 口其他

職級：口企業負責人 口高階主管 口中階主管 口職員 口專業人士

1. 您購買的書籍是？＿＿＿＿＿＿＿＿＿＿＿＿＿＿＿＿＿＿

2. 您從何處得知本產品？(可複選)

　　　口書店 口網路 口書展 口校園活動 口廣告信函 口他人推薦 口新聞報導 口其他

3. 您覺得本產品價格：

　　　口偏高 口合理 口偏低

4. 請問目前您每週花了多少時間學英語？

　　　口 不到十分鐘 口 十分鐘以上，但不到半小時 口 半小時以上，但不到一小時

　　　口 一小時以上，但不到兩小時 口 兩個小時以上 口 不一定

5. 通常在選擇語言學習書時，哪些因素是您會考慮的？

　　　口 封面 口 內容、實用性 口 品牌 口 媒體、朋友推薦 口 價格口 其他＿＿＿＿

6. 市面上您最需要的語言書種類為？

　　　口 聽力 口 閱讀 口 文法 口 口說 口 寫作 口 其他＿＿＿＿＿

7. 通常您會透過何種方式選購語言學習書籍？

　　　口 書店門市 口 網路書店 口 郵購 口 直接找出版社 口 學校或公司團購

　　　口 其他＿＿＿＿＿＿

8. 給我們的建議：＿＿＿＿＿＿＿＿＿＿＿＿＿＿＿＿＿＿＿＿＿＿＿＿＿＿＿＿

＿＿＿＿＿＿＿＿＿＿＿＿＿＿＿＿＿＿＿＿＿＿＿＿＿＿＿＿＿＿＿＿＿＿

喚醒你的英文語感！

Get a Feel for English !

喚醒你的英文語感！

Get a Feel for English !